An Unjust Court

Rodney Smith & Linda Hoagland

DEDICATION

A few days before my friend, Rodney Smith, passed away he called me to request that I finish his book. Of course, I said yes. It never occurred to me, at that time, that his days were so close to ending. I truly thought he would be able to complete the process himself.

This is the book that Rodney and I wrote and it is dedicated to:

RODNEY SMITH

Rodney Smith & Linda Hoagland

ACKNOWLEDGMENTS

Leota Smith, Rodney's lovely wife, allowed Linda Hoagland to finish Rodney's book as he requested.

Victoria Fletcher, fellow author, for editing and formatting this book. She also developed the cover design for the book.

Rodney Smith & Linda Hoagland

CHAPTER 1

SOMETHING TO CELEBRATE

The sun reflected off the giant picture window in the old brick farm house. It was nestled back off the dusty road just enough to give those who passed by from time to time a feeling of somewhere to find solace from the hustle and bustle of the big city of Richmond, Virginia. Long standing oak trees stood on each side of the house. The expansive yard was well-groomed and decorated with rose bushes along with a variety of summer flowers neatly placed throughout the yard.

This house was the gift of a loving husband who married the lady of his dreams and worked each day in the city of Richmond to keep his wife's dreams fulfilled.

Jeffery Logan's father, Harold, spent years grooming his son to take over running the investment firm that Harold had taken from a small office in Henrico County to a two-story building right in the center of the business district of Richmond. In fact, he had refused to agree with his wife, Kathryn, to have any more children after Jeff was born on April 15, 1975.

Jeff, as most people called him, was the apple of his father's eye from the day he was born. He spent many years lavished with expensive gifts and strangely, that excess had not made him arrogant; instead he was very giving to those in need. The summer he turned ten years old, his father gave him a new bicycle and a day later, upon seeing Jeff riding his old bicycle, he demanded an explanation.

Jeff informed him that he had given it to a school friend, who came from an indigent family. When he found out his friend had cancer and wasn't expected to live much longer, he gave his bike to him.

Jeff, being shoved off to Harvard, left Kathryn, a lonely woman in a big house with little compassion from her husband, Harold. Her slender figure, long blonde hair, gentle smile, and a personality that would light up in a room full of people, left her puzzled as to why Harold thought more of his business and less of her. When they wed in May of 1973, a very confident young man wearing a three piece suit announced to all he met that the love of his life had been found upon meeting Kathryn, a business consultant, who frequented some of the same restaurants he did around Richmond.

This day, June 19, 2014, was supposed to be a big day in the lives of the Logan family. Jeff was chosen by his father to take over running the investment firm known as Logan and Son Investments. Jeff loved his father but wondered if he would be able to balance the everyday grind of being fully in charge of the investment firm and keeping his commitment to his wife, Ann. He promised Ann that he would make sure to spend time at home sharing the load of raising their son, Matthew, who had just turned eight years old.

Ann came from a close knit family which included three sisters and two brothers who kept in touch with each other on a weekly basis by phone. They had family outings from time to time, too. Her first fear when she met Jeff was that he would be disappointed in seeing a chubby lady instead of a slender lady, to which he responded after their first date, "That means there's more to love."

Ann had given up her successful real estate business when Matthew was born to stay at home and cherish every moment of raising him. Jeff's taking over his father's business would be a new step in the lives of the Logan family.

"Come on, Ann, you have rearranged everything on the dining room table twice now," Jeff teased while reaching over and dipping his finger into a bowl of French gravy.

"Jeffery Carl, you stop that right now," said Ann.

"You know, Ann, we don't need to go to a big fuss over this."

"Hush, I hear footsteps on the front porch. Go see who it is," scolded Ann.

Before Jeff could open the door, Ann's sister, Kay, and her husband, Melvin, walked in with bowls and trays of food.

"I told you not to bring anything but yourself, Kay," Ann grinned while helping to set the bowl and trays of food on the table.

"I couldn't help wanting to bring you some of our momma's homemade style rolls and Matthew's favorite pudding. By the way, where is he right now," asked Kay.

"He's upstairs studying one of my old real estate books so he will be ready to take his test for his real estate license someday," said Ann.

"Oh my gracious, Ann, he is going to be just like you someday," said Kay.

"And just who are we talking about," a lady with a beautiful smile, medium build, and long, flowing red hair asked as she embraced Ann.

9

"Olivia, it's good to see you again. Where is that handsome husband of yours today," asked Ann.

"He had to go out of town on business, but he sent his best wishes to you all," said Olivia.

"Well, is everybody going to stand there and leave me at the door in this dang wheel chair," asked a loud voice.

"Dad, it's so good to see you and momma here today," Jeff said as he wheeled his dad into the living room with his mother following close behind.

"Ann, get them something to drink and I'll help dad move to my big easy chair for now," said Jeff.

"Oh, momma, you don't look a day older," Jeff gushed as he hugged her.

"Maybe it's all that money of mine she spends at the beauty shop that makes her look so nice," Harold added while chuckling out loud.

"Don't pay any attention to him, son. He gets his perks from Sal's Restaurant three times a week," Kathryn teased.

"Well, maybe I shouldn't have brought my old-fashioned spaghetti today," said a lady with beautiful brown eyes and features that would leave no doubt that she was Ann's mother, Darlene. She giggled as she entered the living room with her hands full of bags and trays of steaming hot food.

"It looks like just about everyone is here today, so I will not be long winded on what I have to say before we eat this beautiful and great smelling food that has been prepared by our loved ones," said Jeff.

"When have you ever been at a loss for words, Jeff," Kay's husband, Melvin said as he watched the expression on Jeff's face.

"I want to thank you all for coming today. I want to thank my gracious wife, Ann for organizing all of this for today. Next, I would like to thank my momma and dad who have put up with me while I was growing up and trying to find my way in life. By the way, I'm not the one who wrapped toilet paper in the trees on the front yard of the mayor's house on Halloween 1985." After thunderous laughing by all gathered there, Jeff continued, "I'm thankful for such a loving family who has supported me through the years. Now, with dad retiring, I have some big shoes to fill. I can say from years ago as a boy trying to fill my father's shoes, I stumbled along and fell to the floor. That is much of what I have done today in learning the investment business. I hope with what he has instilled in me, it will lead me toward a successful way for the future of Logan and Son's Investment Firm.

"You will do well, my son. Now, no more speeches. Let's get in the dining room and eat some of that great food," Harold said while Jeff helped him get into his wheelchair and rolled him to the dining room table.

Once everyone had eaten and enjoyed the company by all, including Matthew who did a comedy skit for them, they slowly began to leave. No words were said by Harold before leaving except a firm handshake with Jeff as Kathryn wheeled him out of the house.

CHAPTER 2

FIRST DAY IN CHARGE

"Jeff, see what is keeping Matthew from getting ready for school," Ann shouted from the bottom of the stairs hoping to hear someone respond to her many calls to breakfast before everyone headed out and on their way for the day.

"He's on his way," Jeff answered while running down the long flight of stairs and kissing Ann as he headed for the door.

"You mean you're not going to take the time to eat breakfast before you head out to work," Ann asked with a disappointed look on her face.

"I have too much to catch up on at the office since dad will no longer be there to help take up the slack in running the business. On top of all that, I have the first day jitters like someone starting a new job," explained Jeff.

"I don't have time either, mom," Matthew said as he hugged her and followed his dad out the door.

Within minutes the house became so quiet that Ann turned on the television in the den and set about getting ready for a busy day. Ann had recently taken a class in learning to abstract paint

12

which helped to relieve the boredom of doing household chores.

Around noon, a chill ran down her spine as she finished a painting she had been working on for several days. She nervously picked up the phone and called Jeff.

"Hello? Jeff?"

"Ann, is something wrong?"

"I'm not sure. I was working on my painting when all of a sudden a chill ran down my spine. I wanted to make sure you were all right," Ann tearfully said.

"Do I need to come home and try to help you settle down?"

"No, you've got enough to deal with right now with taking over the family business."

"Call a sister or friend to come over for a while. If you need me, I will be there at a moment's notice," Jeff said nervously.

"I know you would, Jeff. I will be all right in a little while," she said as she clutched the phone like it was about to get away.

Not even an hour had passed until the doorbell rang. She stopped a few steps from the door and another chill ran down her back. Her thoughts were, *"Could it be woman's intuition?"* She slowly opened the door to find a man dressed quite well with an envelope in his hand.

"Is this the residence of Mr. and Mrs. Jeffery Logan?"

Ann placed her hand over her mouth and waited to hear what he may say next.

"Are you Ann Logan?"

"Yes I am," she nervously said.

"I'm here to serve you with this," he said while handing

13

her the envelope.

"Wait a minute, mister," she shouted after glancing through the papers in the envelope.

"Hey lady, take it up with the court. I did my job," he angrily said while walking toward a car parked in front of the house.

Ann's knees almost buckled as she read the words, Jeffery Carl Logan and Ann Karrie Logan are here by ordered to appear in Juvenile and Domestic Court in Richmond, Virginia, on July 10, 2014, at ten o'clock that morning for a hearing before Judge Henry Abbots to determine that said child, Matthew Harold Logan is the biological son of the above Jeffery Carl Logan and Ann Karrie Logan, residing at 4910 Ridgeway Road, Richmond, Virginia.

Ann trembled as she read the date to appear in Juvenile Domestic court and wondered why someone thought they were not the biological parents of what she and Jeff knew beyond a shadow of a doubt was of their own flesh and blood.

The paper in her hand began to make a crinkle sound as she nervously held it with both hands while walking over to the sofa and falling backwards landing on the soft cushions as she screamed, "Who would want to take the love of our lives away from us?"

With Jeff so busy running the investment firm, she refrained from calling him and instead called her mother, Darlene.

"Hello, this is Darlene Morse."

"Oh mom, I'm so glad to hear your voice."

"What's the matter, Ann? You sound troubled."

"Mom, there was a man who stopped here today and served me with papers stating that Jeff and I will have to go to court for a hearing to determine if we are the biological parents of Matthew,"

Ann said as her bottom lip quivered while she was taking deep breaths.

"Why, what kind of nonsense is that," her mom asked as she nervously waited for an answer from Ann.

"It says Jeff and I have to appear in Juvenile and Domestic Court on July 10, 2014," said Ann.

"Have you talked to Jeff about it," Darlene tearfully asked.

"No, I know he is snowed under with paperwork and trying to get his footing running the company without his dad," said Ann.

"I don't think he would want you to agonize over what you just found out. Give him a call and get back with me as soon as you can," said Darlene.

"I will, mom," Ann sobbed after ending the call.

She wiped tears from her eyes and started tapping in the investment firm number on her cell phone. Within a few moments, that seemed like forever, Jeff answered her call.

"What's wrong, Ann? Did Matthew get hurt? Are you okay?"

"No, I believe he is okay, I'm okay, too. Oh no, I'm not," she said before erupting with sobbing sounds that made her unable to continue talking to him.

"Try to calm down some and explain to me what is happening," Jeff urged, now wondering what would have upset her so.

"Jeff, a server has been here today with papers stating that we have to appear in Juvenile and Domestic Court on July 10, 2014, to determine if we are the biological parents of Matthew."

"Who came up with such a stupid idea," Jeff replied while anger was building up in him like a giant volcano erupting with hot

15

lava spewing in every direction.

"I don't know. I couldn't find a name other than ours and Matthew's," Ann replied between sobs.

"I thought they would have to state in the paperwork you received who filed a petition for custody of Matthew," shouted Jeff.

"I wondered about that, too. I'm a nervous wreck and I hate to have to bother you, but Matthew is our pride and joy," said Ann.

"I will call our attorney and friend, Joe Richards, and have him check into this right away. Be ready to meet me at his office, if need be, in a few minutes. I have been training Becky Millar who has worked for dad and me for years as assistant manager of the office. I will turn it over to her if Joe can work us into his busy schedule," said Jeff.

"I will be dressed and waiting for your call," said Ann as the sobbing had come to a complete stop.

Ann rushed to the bathroom, washed up a bit, put on some makeup, slipped on a dress from her closet, and ran to the front porch where she stood with her cell phone in her hand anticipating that any moment Jeff would call.

Sure enough, within fifteen minutes her phone began ringing.

"Oh Jeff, I thought you would never call me back," Ann blurted out as she wiped tears from her eyes.

"Joe managed to squeeze us in between his appointment with B & S Banking and Rexall's Coal Inc. He could only spare thirty minutes, so be ready to jump into the car when I get there."

"I will be ready and standing in the road when you get here," Ann assured him.

CHAPTER 3

UNSETTLING NEWS

Jeff picked up Ann who was standing on the road in front of the house.

"Try to calm down, Ann, you know Doctor Adams told you your worrying about Matthew, since he was diagnosed with pneumonia shortly after birth, has contributed to your high blood pressure," Jeff urged as he raced down the road at just a little over the speed limit.

It didn't take long before he pulled his car into the parking lot of the Joe Richards Law Firm. Ann immediately jumped out of the vehicle and started walking briskly along the sidewalk leading to the front door of the office.

"Ann, how about slowing down and waiting for me? If you go running in there without calming yourself down first, you will be in the hospital before the day is over," admonished Jeff.

"I can't calm down knowing my son may be taken away from me," Ann responded.

"He's my son, too, you know," Jeff said as he tried to stay

17

calm.

"I'm sorry, Jeff. Please pray I don't go all to pieces if Joe says we may have to give Matthew up to someone and we have no idea who they may be," Ann sobbed as they entered the office.

"Hello, may I help you with something," a young lady sitting behind a big wooden desk asked.

"Yes, I believe you can. I'm Jeff Logan and this is my wife, Ann. We are here to see Attorney Joe Richards."

"Oh yes, I see your names right here scheduled at…. let me see, oh yes, he worked you in for two o'clock. You're right on time. Have a seat and I will let him know you're here," she said as she picked up the receiver and called him. "He said for you to come on in," she announced.

A slightly bald man with a folder in his hand walked past Jeff and Ann as they entered Joe's office.

"I'm sorry to bother you, Joe, on such short notice," said Jeff apologetically.

"That's okay, Jeff. I just finished talking to the man you saw leaving the office. I think you've pretty well filled me in on what you have found out from the letter a server delivered your wife," he said as he turned toward Ann and extended his hand, "I don't think I have seen you since I have been handling your husband's legal problems."

"It's good to meet you, Counselor Richards," said Ann politely.

"You, too, Ann. Now, let's go over what I have found out since talking to you, Jeff," Joe said as he pulled up some information on a computer sitting on his desk. "With the information Jeff has given me over the phone, I did some checking into this and here is what I have come up with. A Nathaniel Arnold and Margaret Lillian Stevens have filed in court a motion

18

to have their biological son returned to them following the investigation of births at Hyeres Medical Center in Richmond."

"How in the world did they come up with this cock and bull story," Ann bellowed while gripping the edge of the desk and staring at Joe with a distraught look on her face.

"It is about the child they thought was theirs when they left the Hyeres Medical Center on June 11, 2006. They found out the truth when the child became sick in 2012 and was diagnosed with the early stages of renal disease. It came to the point that he needed a kidney. Nathaniel Arnold and Margaret Lillian Stevens were DNA tested proving that there was a 99.1% probability they were not the parents of said child James Ray Stevens."

"Oh no, are you saying our child may have been switched with the child of this couple," asked Ann.

"That's what I have found out so far from talking to their lawyer, Martin Hazelton, and what little information the Hyeres Medical Center could give me since their lawyer filed with the court suing the Hyeres Medical Center for negligence in not following guidelines so chartered by the medical center to make sure each child leaves there with his or her biological parents."

"What should we do next to clear this up, Joe," Jeff asked as he fidgeted with his tie.

"You will need to set up an appointment with a lab to do your own DNA testing and let's hope the child you have with the results of the tests proves it is not your child that was switched. There were three other children born that same day."

Ann broke down into tears and then, as Jeff took her in his arms, she fainted.

"Jeff, we'll lay her down on the sofa over there," Joe blurted out as they carried her to the sofa.

"Ann, can you hear me. Oh, please wake up and talk to

me, darling," Jeff pleaded as he wiped perspiration off of her forehead.

"I'm so sorry I passed out. I…" sputtered Ann.

"That's okay. I understand what a shock it is to hear what Joe just found out about who we thought was our precious son," Jeff responded while having her sip some water from a cup Joe handed him.

After taking a few sips, she set the cup down on a table beside her and shouted in an angry way, "Don't give up hope yet, Jeff. He still may be our son."

"I'm not but…" sputtered Jeff.

"Yeah, I know what you're going to say. We've got to be practical and not set our goals too high," said Ann with a hint of sarcasm.

"Okay, so I use my business skills to accomplish other things than running an office efficiently. Try to be patient, Ann. We will get through this some way, but you will need to not let your health deteriorate in the meantime," said Jeff defensively.

"Jeff, why don't you go ahead and take Ann home and let her get some rest. I will do my best to help you clear this up. I have a client I have to represent in court tomorrow, but I assure you, I will be working on this in the meantime," said Joe in firm tones.

"I know you will, Joe. I will talk to you later," Jeff said as he helped Ann up off the sofa and started walking toward the door. Once they were in the car, Ann grabbed Jeff by the arm nearly causing him to hit an oncoming car.

"I don't want to go home right now. Let's go to the hospital and see if they can do the DNA test today," Ann said.

"I don't think they could work us in that quickly," Jeff advised as he pulled the car back onto their side of the road.

"Who are you calling," she asked tugging at his arm.

"I know a clinic that does genetic DNA testing. Dad had an employee who worked for him once who got into a bad relationship and needed to know if he was the father of the baby of the lady he once went with. She had filed for child support," explained Jeff.

Ann sighed.

"Hello, is this Health Labs of Richmond, Virginia," asked Jeff.

"Yes it is. How may we help you," asked a professional female voice.

"This is Jeffery Logan and I would like to set up an appointment for a genetic DNA testing for my wife, son, and I. We…" he said before being interrupted.

"Tell them we want an appointment as soon as possible," Ann whispered.

"We would like an appointment right away. Money is no object," Jeff added while waiting for a reply.

"Mr. Logan, we can work you in at ten o'clock tomorrow morning if that is okay," asked the professional female voice.

"Yes, yes, that will be fine. We will see you tomorrow. Thanks so much," gushed Jeff.

"Jeff, I was just thinking. How are we going to break the news to Matthew," Ann sobbed.

"I have an idea. Until we find out for sure if he is our biological son…" said Jeff.

"What do you mean if," Ann interrupted as she pounded on his arm making him jerk free from her grasp to keep from swerving into the path of a car heading in the opposite direction.

"Let me explain my plan. We will tell him we need to take a test to find out if there is anything he might be subject to inherit from you or me," Jeff suggested.

"That will scare him to death, Jeff," Ann blurted out as she wrung her hands.

"I think that would be better than just coming out and saying we are taking him for a test to see if he is really our son," Jeff responded.

"Jeff, I'm so sorry about how I have acted," Ann cried out as Jeff pulled in the driveway of their house.

"We will get through this, Ann, we just have to keep level heads so we can fight for what is our precious son," he said as he helped her to the sofa to lie down.

Jeff grabbed his cell phone and headed for the kitchen for a snack and a cup of warmed over coffee. The day seemed to drag on and on. Every so often he would glance at the big clock on the wall over the sink.

"Dad, what's wrong with mom," Matthew asked as he tugged at his dad's arm after walking in the kitchen.

"It's just been a tiring day for your mom, Matthew. How about grabbing a snack and going up to your room to finish your homework. She should be feeling better by then," Jeff said as he gave Matthew a hug.

Matthew grabbed a granola bar from the cabinet, poured himself a glass of milk, and began tiptoeing from the kitchen to go upstairs to his room, which brought a smile to Jeff's face as he watched his son's actions.

The evening was spent with Jeff and Ann trying to keep Matthew from noticing how upset they were. Ann fixed one of Matthew's favorite meals: macaroni and cheese with chocolate ice cream for dessert. A few games were played by Jeff and Matthew on their Xbox and then it was bedtime.

"Ann, you did a great job of keeping Mathew from noticing how upset you were from the news you received today," Jeff said while he crawled beneath the blankets on their bed and wrapped an arm around Ann as they tried to settle down for the night.

A few minutes after she turned off the light setting on a table next to the bed, she raised up and asked Jeff, "Did you call the school and let them know Matthew wouldn't be there tomorrow?"

"Yes. Everything is set for tomorrow, so try to settle down and get some sleep," Jeff advised as he held her close to him.

CHAPTER 4

FACING THE ODDS

Facing Matthew early the next morning and trying to keep their composure while telling him a lie was one of the biggest challenges Jeff and Ann had ever faced.

"I don't understand why we have to do this kind of test. Has anybody in the family been affected by a disease that I might inherit from you or mom," Matthew asked why as he finished off a bowl of cereal and looked at Jeff and Ann like they had lost their minds.

"Well, no, uh your uncle Fred on my side had cancer and died from it, but he was ninety nine years old," Jeff responded as he tried to keep from blurting out what the real reason was.

"Matthew, go upstairs, brush your teeth, and get ready to go with us to the lab. Don't put on one of your old shirts and pants. Put on the outfit I laid out for you," Ann shouted as she leaned against the railing of the staircase.

Matthew quickly made his way up the stairs to his bedroom.

"Why is everyone so quiet," Matthew asked as Jeff gripped the steering wheel and Ann bit her nails during the drive to the lab.

"We're just tired, Matthew. Things like this can tire you out so easily. Remember when we took you to the doctor for what looked like mumps and it turned out to be an abscessed tooth," Ann asked as she reached across the front seat to hold Matthew's hand.

"Yeah. I do. I was really nervous because my friend Rudy had the mumps once and he said it wasn't fun at all," said Matthew sadly.

"Remember how tired you were after getting back home from the doctor's office and the visit to the dentist," she asked hoping to convince him that was why they were so quiet and tired because they were anticipating the visit to the lab.

"Yes, I do, mom. You like to never got me out of bed the next morning to go to school," he giggled.

"Here we are," Jeff said after pulling into the parking lot at the Health Labs DNA Testing Center. "Hey Matthew," Jeff said as they got out of the car. "How about us going to your favorite pizza place this evening?"

"Sounds good to me, dad. Let's just take care of this right now and we can plan our trip for this evening," Matthew said in a much more mature way.

The lab was brightly lit as people in solid white uniforms were walking back and forth from the reception desk to the waiting room, calling out people's names and escorting them to one of the many rooms that could be seen from the reception desk.

"Hello, I'm Jeff Logan and this is my wife, Ann, and son, Matthew. We have an appointment with Doctor Larson," Jeff said as he waited for a reply from the young lady sitting behind the desk with a large appointment book spread out in front of her.

"Oh yes, we have you right here," she said while pointing

at the appointment book. "You will need to fill out some paperwork first. You can do that in the waiting room and when you're finished we will call you," she said handing him the paperwork on a clipboard with a pen attached to it. Within a few minutes they had the paperwork filled out and returned to the lady at the reception desk. Ann and Jeffery held hands in the waiting room while Matthew read a magazine.

"Mr. and Mrs. Logan," a lady standing at the door to the waiting room said as she held a clipboard with some papers attached. "Doctor Larson is now ready for you and that handsome young man with you," she teased as Matthew jumped up from where he was sitting and followed them to a room where a doctor was standing as he used a hand held computer.

Upon seeing them he said, "The medical field is so much better with computers today."

"I'm sure it is, doctor," Jeffery said while waiting for an introduction.

"I'm sorry. I'm Doctor Larson and you must be the Logans," he said as he shook hands with both of them.

"I'm Matthew."

"You know, I just figured you might be," Doctor Larson said as a big smile appeared on his face along with a reassuring handshake.

"Okay, Matthew, if you will go with this nice lady, I promise the test she will perform on you will not hurt you," Doctor Larson said as an older lady with a smile on her face gently took his hand and they walked out of the room.

"I understand from what you have written on the paperwork given to you out front that you need testing for proof that you are the biological parents of said child, Matthew Harold Logan," said Dr. Larson

"Yes, we do, doctor, and we want to hold off telling Matthew why we really are being tested until absolutely necessary," Jeff said sternly as he looked eye to eye with Doctor Larson.

"I have handled several of these cases before and hate to say it, but not all parties involved like how they turn out. You do have a lawyer to handle this case," Doctor Larson asked while several laboratory technicians walked in the room to assist him with the test. "We will do swab, fingerprinting, and blood tests to make sure beyond doubt that you and Ann are the biological parents of Matthew Harold Logan. We will immediately send the results to your lawyer as stated on the paperwork you filled out."

Jeff and Ann sat down in Doctor Larson's office while one of his laboratory employees entertained Matthew in another room.

"How long should it take to get the results of the test back, Doctor Larson," Ann asked while biting her lower lip.

"I'll tell you a day or two and it may take us a little longer. I have had some of them take up to two weeks or more…"

"Two weeks or more," Jeff interrupted as he paced the floor and looked as if the weight of the world had just been placed on his back.

"You know we are a very busy laboratory and a lot of people are going through similar circumstances like you are going through," Doctor Larson said as he tried to be up front with them on what they are facing.

"I'm sorry about the way I acted. I'm just so upset at what is taking place now," Jeff said as he reached over and took Ann's hand.

"I understand, Mr. Logan. If you have any other questions, please let us know. I hope you are able to have a good evening. Take care," Doctor Larson said shaking their hands as he walked out of the room with them where they were met by Matthew.

"Are you ready to go home, son," Ann asked as they signed some papers at the receptionist's desk and left.

As days went by, Jeff and Ann began to change from a very loving attitude with each other to being short tempered and having to continuously apologize after outbursts of saying demeaning things to each other. Every time a phone would ring, Ann would grab it and answer it no matter if it was her phone or Jeff's.

"What is taking so long, Jeff? It has almost been two weeks since we took the test and..." asked Ann.

"I'm calling Joe and asking him if he has heard anything lately," Jeff interrupted as he kissed Ann on the cheek while punching in Joe's phone number.

"Joe Richards, Attorney At Law Office, Karen speaking. How may we help you?"

"This is Jeffery Logan and I wanted to talk to him about what he has found out about..."

"Mr. Logan, he just told me to give you a call and make an appointment for you to see him. He is just finishing up with a client right now. Let me put you through to his office," said Karen.

"Jeff, what a coincidence. I just told Karen to give you a call and set up an appointment," said Joe.

"Is it good news or bad, Joe? I don't think Ann nor I could take any more bad news right now," Jeff asked with a voice that sounded weak.

"Hold on a second, Jeff, and let me talk to Karen to see if I have anything open today. I have been so busy with all the cases from the people fighting city hall for damage done to their property by the city which caused flooding on their streets," Joe said hurriedly.

A pause could be heard which just about made Jeff want to

climb the wall as he waited to hear when he and Ann could go to his office.

"Jeff, she just told me that I have an opening at one o'clock if that is okay with you," said Joe.

"That's fine with me. Joe. See you then," Jeff said as he ended the call.

"What did he say," Ann asked as she pulled on Jeff's arm and waited for a response.

"He said we have an appointment to meet him at one o'clock today. He didn't tell me anything he may have found out from the test. We need to get our nerves under control before we go. Did you take your medication the doctor gave you for anxiety disorder," Jeff asked as he wrapped his arms around her.

"Yes I did. I just knew something was going to happen today and I needed all the help I could get to live through what might happen to our precious Matthew," she sobbed and shook in Jeff's arms.

"We will get through this, Ann. I believe our marriage is strong enough to keep us together no matter what..."

"Well, I'm glad you think so," Ann said angrily.

CHAPTER 5

HOPING FOR THE BEST

"Jeff, can't you go a little bit faster," Ann asked impatiently.

"I'm already ten miles per hour over the speed limit and the traffic is terrible this afternoon. Just try to stay calm and don't get upset with Joe no matter what he tells us. He is one of the best lawyers in Richmond," Jeff said while navigating the busy streets on the way to the Joe Richards Law Office.

"I have never seen you without the optimistic attitude that you have now," Ann shouted as she slammed the car door after she stepped onto the parking lot of the law office.

"I'm a realist, too, Ann. We have to brace ourselves for what might not be the best outcome of this situation," Jeff responded as he grabbed Ann's hand when she took off down the sidewalk at a brisk pace.

"Good afternoon. You are the Logans," Joe's secretary, Karen, said as she picked up the phone and punched in a number. "He said to come on in."

"Glad you made it here safe and sound. Have a seat. Would

you like a cup of coffee or tea before we start," Joe asked trying to ease the tension in the air while looking at two distraught people sitting across from his desk.

"No thank you," Ann said with a smug look on her face. "I just want to hear what you found out about our son."

"Okay, here it is. The test came back and the results show that uh… Jeffery Carl Logan and Ann Karrie Logan are 99.7% probability not the biological parents of said child, Matthew Harold Logan," said Joe.

Ann let out a scream so loud that those working in adjoining offices came running into the room to see what had happened. Joe motioned with his hand for them to go back to their offices.

"How could this be, Joe," Jeff asked with his voice quivering.

"I don't believe the test results. Matthew has to be our child. He looks like Jeff and acts so much like me," Ann cried out and pounded on the desk as she shouted. "How could something like this happen to us? We're good people and I'm sure neither one of us has had any secret affairs. For years we have lived and breathed and done everything together because of how much we love each other," Ann cried out as Jeff tried wrapping his arms around her.

"No, don't do that right now. I don't want to be touched by you or anyone while I feel so miserable," she sobbed as she grabbed a tissue out of a box on the desk and wiped her eyes.

"Take one of these, Ann," Jeff said as he handed her one of her anxiety pills.

"All right, but don't expect me to calm down after what I just heard about the test we took," she said as Jeff managed to get her back into the chair at the desk.

"I've called their lawyer after receiving this information and, of course, he was glad for his clients but sorry for what you all are going through now. I have a form for you to fill out, if you will, to send over to the lab giving them permission to send copies of the test results to the Hyeres Medical Center for their evaluation of the test and to the Stevens' lawyer. I will let Hyeres Medical Center know that I will be requesting more information as time goes by," added Joe.

"Thanks, Joe, for what you are doing for us at this time. What is next," Jeff asked.

"I asked the Stevens' lawyer for the test results on Nathaniel Arnold and Margaret Lillian Stevens and the son whom they named James Ray Stevens. Special courier will be bringing that to me anytime now. The child they took home on June 11, 2006, very well may be your son. When I get the results of that information on them, I will send copies to the lab where you took your test. They can check to see for sure," Joe said as he shook Jeff's and Ann's hands when they walked toward his office door. "I will call you as soon as I find out something. I know it's not a good time to discuss this, but you may be able to sue them for negligence," Joe said trying to reassure them of his commitment to them to do all he could for them.

"I don't think there is enough money in the world to mend my heart after what had taken place when I went to have my baby," Ann sobbed as Jeff led her out of the office.

The drive back home was met with sarcastic words and snarled faces shared between them.

A smile came to their faces as they pulled up on the driveway and saw Matthew bouncing a ball on the sidewalk to the house.

"Matthew, I'm so sorry we weren't here when you got off the bus today," Ann said as she hugged him close to her.

"I'm sure glad to see you too, son. We had some business to take care of and it lasted a little longer than we would have liked," Jeff added as he gave Matthew a hug, too.

"Hey, what's with you guys today with all the hugs," he asked seeming confused.

"We're just glad to see you again, Matthew," Ann offered while trying to hold back tears that were forming in her eyes.

"Mom, are you crying," Matthew asked as he held her hand while they walked up the steps of the porch and went into the house.

"It's nothing, Matthew. I just haven't been feeling well lately," Ann said as she tried to keep from crying.

"Is it something to do with those tests? Don't worry, if I come down with one of those diseases, I will fight hard to overcome it. That's what dad and Grandpa Logan taught me," he said as he wiped tears from his mother's eyes.

"I know you would. Now go get cleaned up for supper," she said with her voice soft and affectionate.

"I think I will call the office and make sure everything is going okay, Ann," Jeff said after Matthew headed upstairs to clean up for supper..

"That's fine. I'm going in the kitchen and start supper," she replied.

After a few minutes of talking to his assistant at his office, Jeff heard a sound in the kitchen like a window shattering from being hit with a rock. He immediately ran in the kitchen to see Ann deliberately smashing dishes on the floor.

"Ann, what in the world are you doing," Jeff asked as he grabbed her arm before she could throw another dish to the floor.

"I don't know if I'm going to be able to keep my sanity if I have to give up Matthew," she sobbed as he wrapped his arms around her.

"We will get through this, Ann. It might not be what we want but with each other's love I believe we can go on," he said with his voice quivering. "Let me get a broom and dust pan and get this mess cleaned up before Matthew walks in here and starts asking questions."

Just as Jeff had finished cleaning up the mess from the dishes Ann had broken, Matthew walked into the kitchen.

"I thought I heard a loud noise down here while I was taking a shower," Matthew said as he looked at Jeff and Ann who were trying to not let their emotions show.

"Uh… I dropped a couple plates out of the cabinet and broke them. Your dad just got through cleaning up the mess. Why don't you sit down at the table and I will microwave one of those pizza's you like," she offered hoping to ease Matthew's curious mind.

As the evening wore on, the tension in the air seemed to subside as Jeff, Ann, and Matthew spent their time playing games. They talked about how a vacation spent at Disney World was the most enjoyable time in Matthew's young life.

The hardest thing for Jeff and Ann to do that night was at bedtime when they did the traditional tucking of Matthew into bed for the night. Jeff and Ann took turns hugging him and wishing him a good night's sleep. When they got into their bed, the tension began to build again.

"Jeff, when I hugged Matthew I felt like never letting him go," Ann said as she adjusted the pillow behind her head and pulled the covers up to her chin.

"Huh, what did you say, Ann," Jeff asked as he took off his glasses and laid them on a table beside the bed along with some papers he had been reading.

"How can you lie there looking at that stuff while that precious little boy we love so much may be taken from us," she snarled as she adjusted the pillow again.

"I'll have you know that stuff, as you describe it, is paperwork from the business that puts food on the table and a roof over our heads," he said gritting his teeth and pounding the pillow behind his head in frustration. "I think I love that child just as much as you, Ann. I…"

"Okay, I apologize for how I've acted," she sobbed. "You know you might end up having me committed to a mental ward when all this is settled. Please bear with me."

"I will. Now, let's try to get some sleep," he suggested as he turned off the reading lamp above the bed.

CHAPTER 6

TAKING ONE DAY AT A TIME

"Jeff, Jeff, are you awake," Ann asked as the sun began to filter through the blinds on the windows in their bedroom.

"Yes I am," Jeff answered as he turned over and looked in her direction. "How could I sleep with you tossing and turning most of the night," he said as he turned down the covers on his side of the bed and got up to walk into the bathroom.

"Do you really care," Ann asked as she stood in the bathroom while Jeff shaved his face.

"I wish you wouldn't try to make a contest out of seeing who loves Matthew more," said Jeff.

"I'm sorry, but I feel like you're not…"

"Not as worried about losing the love of our lives. Is that what you mean. Ann," he asked, getting very irritated with her.

"Sorry, Jeff. I will leave you alone and let you get ready for work. I'm going to see if Matthew is up," she said before walking out of the bathroom and heading for Matthew's bedroom.

36

She trembled as she looked at Matthew sleeping in his bed. She slowly walked over to the side of the bed and stood for several minutes just looking at him lying there so peaceful and quiet. Tears begin to roll down her cheeks as she tried to wipe them away with the back of her hands.

"Mom, what are you crying about," Matthew asked as he reached out for her.

"Nothing," said Ann. "I just love you so very much."

"I love you. What is wrong? Have I done something to upset you," he asked trying to figure out why she was crying.

"Heavens no, Matthew. I guess it is because I love you so much and want to see you happy," Ann said.

"I am happy. How could I ask for any two parents to love me more than you and dad do," he sobbed as she held him.

"I know. Now get in the bathroom, take a bath, and get ready for school. I will let you eat your favorite cereal for breakfast this morning instead of insisting on you eating a good hot breakfast," Ann said as she tried to smile.

After Matthew left for school, the house became so quiet that Ann was just about ready to have a nervous breakdown. With trembling hands, she picked up her cell phone and punched in a telephone number.

"Good morning," a familiar voice could be heard by Ann.

"At first, I was going to ask how you knew it was me. Then I realized modern technology has made it possible for anyone to know who is calling," Ann mumbled on, becoming almost incoherent.

"Ann, what is wrong with you?"

"Oh mom, I feel like the whole world is closing in on me,"

she sobbed uncontrollably.

"You've got to get control of yourself. You have to be ready to face this situation with a clear head if you're going to try to keep Matthew," her mom said with a reassuring tone of voice.

"July 10, 2014, is approaching fast and I'm not very optimistic about how it might turn out," Ann said as her voice quivered.

"Is this the girl I raised who sat up all night studying ways to win the history contest in fourth grade? Is this the young lady who was top selling realtor for the state of Virginia for two consecutive years? Is this the…"

"Okay mom, I get your point, but this is different," she countered with a bitter sounding voice.

"How is it different? Yes, we are talking about the little boy we love so much, but it still is the same when it comes to standing up for what you believe in. It's about your lumps and bruises and fighting for what you believe in," her mom said with a very loving tone of voice.

"You're right, but I've been thinking about never tucking him in at night and giving him a big hug," Ann said as she tried to regain her composure. "We only have a week now to prepare for the hearing and I hope you are there that day, mom."

"I will be there along with all your brothers and sisters and don't forget Jeff's family will be there for support. Sorry that your father can't be there. You know you helped me get through the death of your father when he passed away in 2008. Now, you go clean house, go shopping, or call your sisters and brothers. Do whatever it takes to stay busy so you will not have time to dwell on it," her mom advised.

"Thanks, I will," said Ann.

After ending the call, Ann dragged out the vacuum cleaner

and started vacuuming the carpet in the living room when her cell phone began to ring. Looking at the screen, she noticed it was Jeff calling.

"Hello, Jeff. What in the world are you calling about this early in the day," she asked while getting nervous and having to sit down to keep her knees from knocking together.

"Joe just called and said he had the test results on the Stevens' family and could see us in about twenty minutes. Can you be ready by the time I get from my office to the house," Jeff asked.

"Yes, yes, just as soon as you mentioned Joe's name I ran and grabbed a pair of casual pants and shirt. I will put my make-up on while I'm standing near the gate out front," Ann said as she took deep breaths to help keep her calm.

"Great, I will see you in a few," said Jeff.

Ann became much more nervous as Jeff seemed to be taking longer than she expected for him to drive from his office to the house.

The sound of Jeff's car could be heard before she could see his car speeding up the long winding road to their house. Within a minute, Ann was in the front seat beside Jeff and they started their journey toward Joe's office.

"Fast enough for you, Ann," Jeff asked as he pulled into a parking spot next to Joe's office.

"You did well," Ann said as they hurried up the sidewalk and into the office of their lawyer, Joe Richards.

"Good morning, how are you two holding up so far," Joe's secretary asked as they stood in front of her desk.

"Not too well, Karen, but we will survive," Jeff said while trying to smile but finding it hard to do so.

"I will tell him you're here. I 'm sure he will take you right in because he has been working hard to catch up enough on his other clients to make room for you today," she said as she picked up the phone to call him. "You can go on in now," she said as they started walking toward his office.

"I'm sorry I hadn't called you sooner but the courier was late and I didn't get the information until this morning. Have a seat and I will go over with you what the Stevens' lawyer sent me," he said as he picked up some papers from his desk and proceeded to read from them.

"It states that the test results from Carlton Laboratories of Richmond has found that Nathanial Arnold Stevens is not the father of James Ray Stevens nor Matthew Harold Logan and…"

"What are you saying, Joe," Jeff asked.

"Well, here is the kicker. Their lawyer, Martin Hazelton, was holding back on us, which is a strategy that lawyers will use to get an advantage sometimes. The couple have separated but Mr. Arnold still wants to be involved. He is probably hoping to collect some money from the suit they filed against Hyeres Medical Center," Joe explained.

"What about Margaret Lillian Stevens," Ann asked as she held onto the arms of the chair she was sitting in so hard that her knuckles were turning red.

"I'm sorry to say but the DNA test shows that Margaret Lillian Stevens is the biological mother of…"

"Please don't say it. Oh please, don't tell me I'm not the biological mother of Matthew," Ann sobbed as Jeff worked to restrain her from throwing the chair she was sitting in across the room.

"I'm afraid I will have to tell you that the DNA test states that she is 99.9% the mother of the child that you have been raising and have named Matthew Harold Logan. DNA test results taken on

40

the child she has raised after the mix up at Hyeres Medical Center show the DNA test match those of Jeffery Carl Logan and Ann Karrie Logan. Sad to say, but the child they were raising as James Ray Stevens died from renal failure a week ago," continued Joe.

Ann jerked free from Jeff's grasp on her and started twisting her hair and crying out, "I don't want to live now that I know my biological son is dead and the boy I raised will soon be taken away from me."

"Mrs. Logan, please don't give up yet. We may be able to convince the judge to make some kind of joint custody agreement," Joe urged as he stood next to Jeff and Ann.

"It just will not be the same. I love Matthew so much and I don't know how to handle what you just told me," Ann sobbed while looking like she could faint any minute.

Joe looked directly at Ann and said, "I believe it's time you told Matthew the situation he may have to face soon."

"How do you tell a little eight year old that he is not our child and that our child lived with someone else and died," Jeff asked while raising his voice.

"That's got to be tough to do. I have two children of my own and I don't know how to tell you to handle that. You may need to consult a psychiatrist for some help with that," Joe offered.

"No, I think Jeff and I are capable of handling it because we love him dearly even if he isn't part of our flesh and bones," Ann softly said as she wiped tears from her eyes with a tissue.

"Very well, I will continue preparing for the hearing and if I hear of anything that I need to go over with you in the meantime, I will call you. Have you considered taking legal action against the medical center," Joe asked while walking them to the front door of his office.

"No, not yet. We are still thinking about it," answered Jeff.

As they were driving home, Ann glanced at her cell phone.

"Jeff, I just noticed a call on here from the court," Ann said as she was retrieving the message and listening to it.

"What did it say," Jeff asked.

"It asked us to call for an appointment to be set up to talk to Matthew, you, and me. It is authorized by the Juvenile and Domestic Court to arrange for a visit from a child psychologist. She asked if tomorrow at nine o'clock in the morning would be okay. If it is, we're to call and leave a confirmation of the acceptable date." Ann said as she looked toward Jeff who was gripping the steering wheel with his arms rigid and perspiring heavily.

"Yes, it is. I will call the office and let them know I will not be there in the morning," Jeff nervously said.

"Jeff, I'm so sorry you have had to miss so much work because of this," Ann sobbed.

"Sweetheart, it's for a good cause. I will call the school and let them know about Matthew having to be here for the child psychologist. We need to prepare for what we are going to say to Matthew when he comes in from school this evening," Jeff said as he parked the car in the driveway of their house.

"We only have a few minutes before Matthew gets home from school. I don't know if I…" said Ann.

"We can do this. I admit it will not be easy, but we have to think of Matthew's well-being most of all," Jeff softly said.

After phones calls were made and a quick freshening up in the bathroom, Jeff and Ann sat in the living room like they were sitting on needles.

"We can do this," Jeff murmured as they heard the school bus pull up in front of the house. Panic set in as they heard the sounds of footsteps and the opening of the door.

"Matthew, it is so good to see you," Jeff said while forcing a smile to his face hoping to keep Matthew from sensing the pain he was feeling from the thought of having to tell him he was not their child.

"Good to see you and mom here at the same time today," Matthew grinned as he took his back pack off, laid it on the coffee table, and then hugged his mom.

"Matthew, we have something that we need to discuss with you right away," Jeff said stiffly.

"What is it? Billy wants me to come over to his house to see his new Xbox game in a little while," Matthew responded with a puzzled look on his face.

"Please come over here and sit on the sofa between your dad and me," Ann murmured trying so much to keep from crying.

"Okay, here I am," Matthew said as he plopped down on the sofa between them.

Jeff starts first, "Matthew, remember the test we all took?"

"Yes. Oh no, don't tell me I'm going to come down with some terrible disease and not be able to go to college someday," Matthew said jokingly.

"No, it's nothing like that son," Ann countered. "We took the test to determine if we are…" Ann broke down and started crying.

"What's the matter," Matthew asked while wrapping his arms around her.

"Let me try to explain," Jeff said with his voice quivering. "You remember us telling you several years ago how your mom carried you around inside of her for a while and then she went to the medical center and you were born?"

"Yes. What is this all about that has made mom and you so upset," Matthew asked looking very emotional and starting to form tears in his eyes.

"I know this isn't a good comparison to what I'm going to tell you, but remember the time the clerk got mixed up at the store and gave you the wrong pair of shoes that we had bought for you," Jeff asked as he searched for the right words to use.

"Yes, but you took them back and got the right size later on," Matthew answered seeming very confused.

Ann reached over to cup her hands around Matthew's face and said, "Matthew, there was a mix up at the medical center and we took the wrong baby home."

"Are you telling me I'm like that pair of shoes that got mixed up at the store? I'm not really your son," he cried out, jumped up off the sofa, and took off to his room crying.

"Jeff, let me go talk to him and see if I can say the words that will not cause him to panic and who knows what else," Ann said as she walked toward Matthew's room.

"Matthew, may I come into your room?" Ann asked while softly knocking on the closed door.

"It is your house, not mine. Do what you want to do," a muffled voice cried out.

"Oh Matthew, this is hurting your dad and I just as much as it is hurting you. We had no idea there had been a mix up at the medical center. Regardless, whether or not you're of our flesh and bones, we're going to love you forever and try our level best to keep you with us," Ann said as she wrapped her arms around Matthew and wiped the tears off his cheek with a tissue.

"I don't want to live with someone else. I want to live

with…."

"Go ahead and say it. I want you to call us mom and dad no matter what happens," Ann said while brushing the hair out of his eyes.

"What are you going to do to make sure you can keep me forever, mom," he asked as he settled down some.

"First of all, we have to talk with a lady who will be here in the morning. She will probably ask questions about how we treat you and check out your room to see how clean it is. Young man, I want you to clean your room, get your homework finished, and be ready for supper in about an hour," she replied with a smile on her face.

"What will happen after we talk to the lady tomorrow," Matthew asked with a serious look on his face.

Ann studied him for a minute and then said, "Remember those court shows your daddy and I watch?"

'Yes. I've watched a few of them," he said wondering what she would say next.

"We all have to go to court July 10th, five days from now. They will decide, what we believe, that you will be allowed to stay with us," Ann said not really knowing how it would turn out that day but trying hard to keep Matthew from getting really upset.

"I'll get started on my room," he chuckled while picking up books and toys off of the floor.

"How did it go, Ann," Jeff asked as she sat down on the sofa next to him and held his hand.

I believe we will be okay for now. I told him a lady would be here in the morning to talk to us about how we treat him and how clean his room is. I told him we would have to go to court a week from today so they can decide if we can keep him. I told him

I believe they would let us keep him and…."

"You have no idea how it is going to go at the hearing. Why did you lie to him," Jeff countered as he looked down at Ann with a frown on his face.

"I couldn't tell him we just might not be able to keep him," she sobbed.

"I understand, Ann. I will order a pizza for supper tonight so you don't have to cook," he tenderly said.

"Thanks for understanding. I sure hope things work out for the best or I may lose my mind. I'm going to go call my sisters and brothers and fill them in on what we know so far," said Ann.

"I'm going to call my folks and tell them what we found out so far," Jeff said as he sat down on the sofa while holding his cell phone.

CHAPTER 7

PREPARING FOR A VISIT

Jeff and Ann spent the next day at the park enjoying a picnic lunch with Matthew. Early the next morning was filled with cleaning the house and preparing for the visit with the child psychologist.

"Matthew, I laid out an outfit for you to wear today and you come walking in the kitchen wearing a pair of your worst looking jeans and shirt. There's even a hole in the left elbow of the shirt. Why did you do that," asked Ann angrily.

"Oh mom," Matthew cried out and took off running upstairs. Ann started to follow him and was abruptly stopped by Jeff who was holding onto her arm.

"Let me go talk to him," Jeff softly said as he started to walk up the stairs. "Matthew, may I come into your room," Jeff asked while knocking on the door.

Matthew was laying on the bed, face down, and sobbing when he mumbled, "I guess."

"Why did you put on those old clothes knowing the child psychologist would be here shortly," Jeff asked as he sat on the bed next to Matthew.

"I thought if I wore some old clothes, the lady would not be tempted to take me to live with someone else," he sobbed.

"Your thought was well-justified in doing so since you thought that would keep you here with us. I want you to know that your mom and I will do everything we can to keep you with us. You need to make a good impression on her when she visits us today," Jeff suggested, looking at Matthew who was sitting up on the side of the bed next to Jeff.

Matthew had a puzzled look on his face when he said, "What do you mean by good impression? I brushed my teeth this morning. Will that work?"

"Son, I mean you need to tell her truthfully how you are treated while living here with us," Jeff responded.

"Do you mean like mom does when some sales lady stops by the house to try to sell her something," he offered for an example.

"Yeah, I guess you could say it is something like that. Your mom and I will treat them friendly and may offer them something to drink or eat. Just be yourself and you will do fine," Jeff said as he watched Matthew's expression change from a frown to a smile on his face.

Matthew nodded and the smile grew bigger.

"Now, get changed and come downstairs to eat some breakfast. By that time, the lady should be here for a visit with us," Jeff said as he walked out of Matthew's room.

Breakfast that morning was spent by saying very few words between them except every now and then Matthew would tell Jeff and Ann something he saw on a children's show the day before. While Ann gathered up the breakfast dishes and put them in the dishwasher, Jeff made sure Matthew hadn't spilled anything on his clothes. Then he asked Matthew to come in the living room and sit with him until the child psychologist arrived.

After what seemed like an eternity, the doorbell rang, sending everyone into a panic knowing it was probably the lady from the state coming to visit them.

Jeff opened the door and a lady who looked to be in her early forties was standing there with a satchel in her hand. Jeff felt a little at ease seeing a beautiful lady with a friendly smile on her face. "Come on in. I'm Jeffery Logan and this is my wife, Ann, and son, Matthew, sitting on the sofa."

"Good to meet you. I'm Cynthia Harper from Juvenile and Domestic Court and as you know I'm here to interview you for the court," she said clearing her throat and trying to ease the tension in the room.

"All right, let's get started," Jeff responded.

"So, how long have you lived here at 4910 Ridgeway Road, Richmond…"

"Is that information necessary for how we have raised Matthew," a frustrated Ann asked as Jeff grasped her hand to try to calm her down.

"Yes, it is, Mrs. Logan," she said as she looked at Ann with a look of disdain.

"Would you excuse us for about a minute, Ms. Harper," Jeff asked as he motioned with his eyes to Ann to leave the living room with him.

"Yes, that will be okay," replied Ms. Harper.

"Ann, you are going to have to calm down or she is going to think you have a terrible temper and that would not be a good thing to have if we want Matthew to stay with us," Jeff whispered to her.

49

"I don't like being questioned, like being interviewed for a job," Ann angrily said. "I'm no nut case, Jeff…"

"Ann."

"All right, Jeff, I will try, but she needs to understand what this precious little boy means to us," she said as she wiped tears from her eyes. She applied lipstick to her lips and looked into a mirror on the wall with a grimace.

"I'm sorry about that, Ms. Harper. Please go ahead with your questions," said Ann.

"Place of residence," she asked.

"Let me answer," Jeff prompted. "We started out living in a modest apartment in Henrico County for a while and then I surprised Ann with this place."

"Would you mind going to your room until your mom and dad talk for a while," Ms. Harper asked Matthew.

"I want to be here to find out what is going to happen to me," Matthew answered while holding tightly to Ann's hand.

"Matthew, I'm here to help you, not hurt you. Please just give us a few minutes to talk and then you can come back at which time I will ask you some questions. After that, I will leave. Okay," said Ms. Harper.

"I guess," he said as he slowly left the room.

"How has it been raising Matthew with your jobs and other commitments," Ms. Harper asked.

"I had a successful real estate business and when Matthew was born, I sold it and stayed home to raise Matthew," Ann said as she looked at her intently.

"I worked my way up in my father's investment firm which grew to a big office building in the heart of Richmond, Virginia.

50

He just recently retired and turned the business over to me," Jeff added.

"Do you feel you allot enough time to do things with Matthew like help with homework, go to a park for a day, and other activities that parents do to share time with their children," asked Ms. Harper.

"Yes, I do, Ms. Harper. Ann and I always make time to do things with him that he likes. We limit his time watching TV before bed time and monitor what he watches. We are firm believers in sharing time with our son," Jeff said while nervously watching Ms. Harper writing down just about everything they had been telling her.

"Now, this question may take a moment for a response due to the content of it. How do you handle a situation where Matthew has done something that may be subject to correction? Let's say, for example, he took a crayon and wrote on a wall in the living room," continued Ms. Harper.

"The first thing we would do is sit him down and explain why it is wrong to do that because it is not something we would be happy with him doing. We then would ask for an apology from him. Then we would take away some of his privileges like no TV, games, riding of his bicycle for a certain amount of time," Ann said as she worked hard to appear calm.

"Very good. Now, would you mind if I take a tour of your house and talk to Matthew by myself," Ms. Harper asked.

"Yes, by all means," Jeff said, watching her as she started walking through the house while writing on a paper on a clipboard.

After several minutes, Ann got up and started to head toward the upstairs where Ms. Harper was.

"Ann, sit back down. It will be over soon," Jeff insisted.

"Okay. I will try my best, but it will not be easy," Ann

whispered.

Both Jeff and Ann began pacing back and forth in the living room and watching the Big Ben clock sitting on the mantle of the fireplace.

"I'm sorry it took so long," Ms. Harper said while walking into the living room holding Matthew's hand. "He wanted to show me his collection of matchbox cars."

"Is there anything else you would like to ask us before you leave, Ms. Harper," Ann asked.

"No, I think I have everything on my list taken care of. I will just say I have enjoyed meeting the Logan family," Ms. Harper replied.

"Thank you for coming, Ms. Harper," Jeff said as he and Ann walked to the door with her.

"Jeff, I'm worn out," Ann said after watching her leave.

"She was a nice lady, mom," Matthew said as he sat down on the sofa beside her.

"What kind of questions did she ask you, Matthew," Ann asked.

"Ann, I don't know if we should go there right now," Jeff said sitting down on a chair next to the sofa.

"It's okay, mom. She just wanted to know if you and dad ever became angry in front of me and if I felt like you all didn't love me. I told them you never argue in front of me and I know you all love me," Matthew replied as he was surrounded by Jeff and Ann.

"Nothing like a family hug is there," Jeff laughed.

The rest of the day for Jeff and Ann was spent trying not to smother Matthew with too much attention which was hard to do.

CHAPTER 8

ONLY TIME WILL TELL

The sound of the doorbell at the front door sent Jeff and Ann into a frenzy as they tried to get their robes on. They headed to the front door to find out who could be ringing their doorbell so early in the morning. Upon opening the door, they were met by a FedEx Worker who was holding a white envelope.

"I have a delivery for Jeffery Logan or Ann Logan," said the delivery man.

"I'm Jeffery Logan," Jeff said while signing for the delivery.

After closing the door, Jeff ripped open the envelope and pulled out a handwritten letter. Seeming confused, they both sat down on the sofa and Jeff started reading aloud what had been written on several sheets of note book paper.

Dear Jeffery and Ann Logan,

> I realize your heart is broken by the news you have received about the son you have raised, telling you that he is not your biological son. How tragic it must be for you now to hear the son you were to go

home with from the hospital after birth is now deceased.

I want you to know how traumatic it was for me to hear that little James Ray Stevens is not my biological child and my husband Nathaniel is not the father of James nor Matthew. Please let me explain myself, about my character, and the kind of life I lived before marrying Nathaniel.

First of all, I drank much too much and hung out at some bars around Richmond. Spending the night at some sleazy hotel was nothing out of the ordinary for me at that time. It just so happened that I fell in love with Nathaniel, one of my regulars to spend the night with. After a few months and with his insistence, I accepted an offer to move in with him.

A few months after we were living together, I began to have morning sickness and mood swings. After discussing it with Nathaniel, we bought a pregnancy test kit and the results showed that I was pregnant.

I will not bore you with everything that has happened up until now, but fill you in on some details that may explain how I feel about the mix up of our children. I would love to meet you before the court hearing if you don't mind. Maybe we can work something out without going through the court hearing on July 10th. I have enclosed my phone number on a business card so you can get in touch with me.

Best Regards,

Lillian Stevens

"What is she trying to pull with us," Jeff asked after folding the letter up and slamming it down on the coffee table.

54

"Maybe she might be willing to let us keep Matthew now, Jeff..." sputtered Ann.

"Are you kidding me? Are you going to believe this bunch of bull," Jeff angrily said.

"It sounds to me like she might have had a change of heart and may feel the best place for Matthew is with us," Ann responded.

"I have heard stories similar to that in my years of dealing with the public and I bet she is smiling while waiting to stick a knife in our backs, so to speak, if we try to keep Matthew," said Jeff bitterly.

"How about we give her the benefit of the doubt," Ann asked while picking up the business card and looking at it.

"No, no, Ann. Give me that card now," Jeff shouted while trying to wrestle the card away from her.

"Let me just hold on to it for a while," Ann suggested as Jeff raised his hands up with a disgusted look on his face.

"Okay, but don't do anything without consulting me first, do you hear me, Ann," he said with a sigh of irritation.

"Okay, Jeff, now let's get Matthew up and I will fix breakfast while you two get ready for your day," Ann said as she smiled at Jeff.

"All right, Ann, you win for now," he said giving her a big hug and a kiss.

"Hey, what's going on in here this morning with you two," asked Matthew.

"Matthew, you're up, dressed, and ready for school already," Ann said as she looked at him standing in the living room staring at them.

"Yeah, look at you two still in your robes and probably no breakfast fixed yet," he said as he laughed at them.

"Matthew, you are much too mature for your age, young man," Jeff laughed while chasing after him with a pillow off of the sofa. Ann giggled as she watched them.

"Okay, Matthew, I will whip up a batch of pancakes while your dad gets ready for work." She grinned while she looked at them wrestling on the sofa.

"Time out, Matthew," Jeff laughed getting up off the sofa. "I need to get ready for work and you need to eat your breakfast and get on that big yellow school bus soon."

"I'll go get started on breakfast…"

"Uh, Ann, I need to get to the office early this morning to catch up on some business, so fix me a cup of coffee to go," said Jeff.

"You got it, Jeff," Ann said as she walked to the kitchen.

Jeff gave a stern warning to Ann to not try to communicate with Lillian Stevens until he had time to talk to Joe about how to handle the situation without jeopardizing their chance to keep Matthew.

Trying to keep from calling the number on the card that Lillian Stevens sent just about got the best of Ann. She cleaned hardwood floors and carpets in the house, washed curtains and re-hung them. Just about noon, her will power to refrain from calling the phone number on the card got the best of her. She opened a drawer on her make-up table, pulled out the business card that Lillian Stevens had written her phone number on, and punched in the number on the card.

"Hello, I just had it in my heart that you would call me soon," a friendly voice said.

"Yes, I'm sure your caller ID picked up our names," Ann softly said while waiting for a reply.

"This is Lillian Stevens and I'm so glad you called, Mrs. Logan."

"You can call me Ann if you like. What do you think we can accomplish by talking to each other before the hearing," Ann asked with apprehension in her voice.

"It just may help us to understand how we both feel about what took place at Hyeres Medical Center. Can you meet me at Roxy's Café, 1104 West Main Street, in about an hour," asked Lillian Stevens.

"Yes, I believe I can do that. I need to call my husband to let him know I'm going to meet you in…."

"I beg you not to call your husband right now if you want to talk about the boys and what we may be able to work out for Matthew," Lillian interrupted.

"Okay, I will see you there in about an hour. How will I be able to recognize you," Ann asked.

"I will wear a blue sweatshirt and baseball hat with the letters for Atlanta Braves on it," said Lillian Stevens.

"Very well, I will see you in about an hour," Ann reluctantly said before ending the call.

CHAPTER 9

FACING THE ODDS

Ann took a deep breath and wondered what meeting Lillian would be like. After trying on several different dresses and pants, she settled for a modest dress and heels. Sweeping back her hair with a brush revealed some gray hair now beginning to show in what Jeff always called her beautiful brown hair. Grabbing her purse and cell phone, she jumped into her car and took off at a high rate of speed.

Luckily the traffic was running smoothly on Main Street as she looked for Roxy's Café, which turned out to be easy to find. After parking a block away due to the busy businesses on Main Street, her stomach began to churn as she opened the door to the café and started looking for someone dressed liked Lillian had described on the phone.

"It's got to be you, Lillian," Ann said as she looked at a lady several years younger than her. Her complexion was ruddy and several scar lines were prominent on her chin. The smell of cigarette smoke was very recognizable for Ann due to the years growing up in a household of smokers.

"Oh yes, it is. It's so good to meet you…" said Lillian.

"Ann."

"Ann, that's right. Please forgive me. I have been such a nervous wreck since finding out about the mix up in our children. I thought…" said Lillian with feigned sincerity.

"Pardon me. Would you like something to drink or eat," a young man in an apron and big smile on his face asked Ann.

"A cup of coffee with cream will be fine. Thank you," she replied curtly.

"Now where was I," Lillian asked after the order was taken by the young man. "Oh yes, the mix up at the hospital has made me a nervous wreck. The son I had been raising as James Ray Stevens was diagnosed with kidney disease and doctors said he might survive with a kidney transplant. Nathaniel and I decided for one of us to be a donor. Needless to say, that is when we found out we were not a match for donating a kidney for James. While we searched for a kidney donor, James died of renal failure. In checking with the hospital, we knew it might be a mix up on babies born the day we were there. Of course, they failed to admit they may have mixed up the births of the babies born that day. We hired a lawyer and as you know, he was able to get a hearing set. Another blow came when your lawyer sent the DNA tests to our lawyer who informed us that I was the biological parent of the child you are now raising."

"What about your husband, Nathaniel, not being the father of the child my husband and I have been raising," Ann asked as she took a drink of the coffee from the cup the young man just set down on the table.

"I was sure he was the father of the child I carried for nine months and gave birth to the same day you gave birth at Hyeres Medical Center. I will admit I was living a promiscuous life back then," Lillian explained while never making eye contact with Ann.

"Do you have any idea who the father might be," Ann

urged trying to understand all that Lillian had just told her.

"Maybe. Not sure," said Lillian.

"Don't you think whoever the biological father is may want to know he has a son living and breathing upon the earth, Lillian," Ann angrily said.

"No," Lillian said raising her voice so loud that just about everyone in the café looked toward where they were sitting which made Lillian blush. "The kind of men I ran around with would take off running as far as they could from me if they thought they might be the father of a child I gave birth to," Lillian ranted while still failing to make eye contact with Ann.

"Do you have any pictures of James with you," Ann asked.

"Oh yes, I have some in my purse. Here, you take a look at these," she said as she handed Ann a wallet with pictures in it.

After several minutes of looking at the pictures in the wallet, Ann almost went into shock seeing a young boy who looked so much like Jeff and wearing a smile like hers.

"Please tell me what he was like," Ann suggested with tears in her eyes.

"He was a curious little child. He would sit and try to read a newspaper long before he was taught how to read. He seemed to get along with just about everyone he met. He loved to listen to music, no matter what kind it was. The teachers at the school he attended said James' test scores were much higher than anyone else in his class. I guess that is just about all I can think of right now. Let's talk about how we can handle this situation with the medical center that may help us both," Lillian suggested.

"Wait a minute," Ann said slightly raising her voice. "You haven't even asked to see any pictures of Matthew or what he is like," she snarled becoming very irritated with the way Lillian was acting.

"I'm sorry. I guess it's all the things that are happening in my life now that I forgot to ask," Lillian mumbled.

"You're pathetic, you know that? Why in the world wouldn't you be chomping at the bit to find out what Matthew is like," Ann fumed, seeing how little emotion was coming from Lillian.

"I do, but…"

"What do you mean by that," Ann insisted.

"Let me get something straight right now, lady. I believe I hold the cards in this game and I intend to win the custody of that child," Lillian angrily said as she pulled her chair closer to where Ann was sitting. "I will love that kid, but I believe the Hyeres Medical Center should have to pay dearly for what they have caused. Don't sit there high and mighty like you have no intentions of collecting a large sum of money from them. I…"

"Is that all Matthew means to you, a big sum of money from the medical center? Why did you want to meet with me? You're telling me you have the upper hand in what is going to happen," Ann said as she held her upset stomach.

"Okay, I will tell you what I wanted to discuss with you. I will agree to allow you to keep the child you have…" said Lillian.

"He's got a name, Lillian," Ann interjected, wanting so much to punch her in the face.

"All right, all right, I will agree to let you and your husband keep Matthew if we can work out a price for you to pay me after you settle your suit with Hyeres Medical Center," said a smug Lillian.

"What? Are you that greedy that you want us to pay you so we can keep him when you will probably get a large sum of money out of the suit with the medical center, too? You know, I think this conversation needs to end right now," Ann said while raising her voice. "Here you go, there is enough money there to pay for my coffee and whatever you had," Ann blurted out while slamming down several dollar bills.

"This is not over yet," Lillian shouted toward Ann as she walked toward the door. "Think it over. You will be sorry in the long run if you fail to take my offer. You hear me, Ann?"

Ann kept on walking toward the door and although she could hear Lillian, she left the café without looking back.

Tears rolled down Ann's cheeks as she ran to her car and threw her purse across the front seat hitting the passenger door. She cried all the way home. After unlocking the front door, picking up the mail from the mail box next to the door, she ran to the living room, and fell on the sofa where she cried herself to sleep.

CHAPTER 10

TAKING A CHANCE

"Mom, are you okay," asked Matthew.

"Matthew, I didn't hear you come in," Ann mumbled as she tried to focus on Matthew who was now standing over her with a concerned look on his face.

"Are you okay," he asked again.

"Yes, I'm….I uh… just fell asleep on the sofa," Ann said hoping he would believe the lie she just told him.

"Why would you take a nap with your coat and shoes on, Mom," he continued to grill her as if he was an adult searching for the truth in what she was saying.

"Let's forget about that. Now, tell me how your day was at school," she asked hoping to change the subject.

"I got an 'A' on a spelling test and I was able to name just about all the states except one," he smiled.

"And what state was that young man," she giggled.

"The same one I forgot about when you studied with me," he laughed.

"You forgot the 49th state." She grinned.

"Yeah, I did. I'm still thankful that I'm in an advanced class of learning," he beamed.

"Anything else happen that you might want to tell your mom about, like that cute little girl you wave at when you get off the bus from time to time," she teased.

"Yeah, there was. When we took our lunch break and after finishing my lunch, Freddy and I went out on the playground to swing. There was a lady standing in front of a car parked on the street across from the playground," he said as he looked at his mom for an explanation.

"She could be looking at one of her children who goes to school there," she offered trying to put his mind at ease.

"I don't think so. She stared directly at me. Every time I would look around she would wave at me and..."

"What did she look like," Ann interrupted, worrying about what may happen in the future with Matthew.

"She was kind of young and smoked cigarettes the whole time she stood there," he said nervously after the questioning by Ann.

"Was there anything else you can remember about her, like the color of her hair or what her face looked like?" Ann wanted to take him and get far away from anyone who could hurt or try to take Matthew away from her.

"She had a scar on her chin but I couldn't make out much about her face because of the hood on the jacket she was wearing," he said as tears filled his eyes. "Mom, is someone trying to catch me and take me away from you and dad," he whispered as he clung to the side of Ann.

"Oh Matthew, we're not going to let anyone snatch you up and take you away from us," she said biting her lower lip. "Now, go do your homework and I will fix you some macaroni and cheese to eat," she said as she watched him climb the stairs to his room.

She then punched in a number on her cell phone.

"Hello, who is calling?"

"You know who this is and I'm only going to tell you this just one time. Stay away from Matthew, do you hear me," Ann shouted as she stood in the living room closet to keep Matthew from hearing her on the phone.

"Oh, did the little brat snitch on me? Let me tell you something, Ann Logan. You are in for a fight, so you better get ready. I was willing to sit down with you today and work out a deal, but you acted high and mighty," the now familiar voice of Lillian shouted into the phone.

"I think I have you figured out, Lillian. You are worried about the upcoming hearing. Just what are you trying to hide that could cause you to fail to gain custody of Matthew," Ann questioned.

"You know you're getting under my skin, lady. You know what happened to a lady who kept at me for dating her boyfriend. I…"

"Oh, so now you're threatening me," Ann asked trying to keep from screaming for fear Matthew would hear her.

"Here is the deal. You can call me anytime up till the day of the hearing and we will work something out or you will probably lose your child in the court hearing to me," snarled Lillian.

"Don't hang up on me," Ann screamed and the only thing

she could hear was silence on her cell phone. After opening the closet door, her heart just about stopped beating because Matthew stood there with a distraught look on his face.

"Mom, you're up to something. You screamed and I took off down the stairs to see what was going on. What are you hiding from me," Matthew demanded as he stared at her with his hands on his hips.

"I'm sorry. I was talking to the lady we have to see in court and we were having a disagreement on something. I didn't want you to be alarmed by my shouting on the phone," Ann said softly while brushing Matthew's hair back out of his face.

"Why were you shouting? I still believe you're hiding something from me and you always told me we shouldn't keep secrets," he said with tears forming in the corner of his eyes.

"I know we taught you that and I've failed to practice that lately. Son, I know you are much more mature than your young age, but some things just can't be explained to you until you're old enough to understand that some people are just hard to deal with. Don't you worry, your daddy and I love you so much and we will do anything to keep from losing you," she said as she tried to comfort him.

"I believe you, Mom, but…"

"Come on now, let's see a big smile on your face," she urged trying so hard to keep from breaking down and crying in front of him.

"Okay, I will try it," he said with a big smile and a hug from Ann.

"Go upstairs and do your homework, young man," Ann giggled as she chased Matthew toward the stairs in a playful way.

She then picked up her cell phone and punched in a number.

"Hello, Joe Richards, Attorney at Law, Karen speaking. How may I help you?"

"Hi Karen, this is Jeff Logan's wife, Ann. I was wondering if Joe could see Jeff and me this evening," Ann asked hoping he would be able to work them in.

"Let me see, Mrs. Logan," she said as she looked at the appointment log on her desk.

"I believe he can work you in at around five o'clock. Let me check with him. Please hold on," Karen said politely.

A few minutes passed and Karen said, "He said that will be fine with him. Anything else you need, Mrs. Logan?"

"No, that will be fine. Thank you so much, Karen," Ann said as she ended the call. She tried to think of a way to tell Jeff that she had met with Lillian Stevens earlier that day. She knew he would be angry that she would do something like that behind his back. She then picked up her cell phone and called her sister, Kay, who only lived a few miles from their house.

"Ann, I've been waiting to hear from you. Mom filled me in on all that has been happening to you and Jeff about Matthew. I…"

"I'm sorry, Kay, I need a favor from you," Ann interrupted as she bit on her lip and tried to calm her nerves.

"You know I would do anything in the world for you. All you have to do is ask," Kay said.

"I need you to keep Matthew this evening while we are at the lawyer's office," Ann responded.

"Sure, I will be glad to keep my nephew anytime. Maybe he can help me learn how to use my new cell phone," Kay laughed. "He is a little genius, you know."

67

"How about coming over here at about four thirty," suggested Ann.

"Sounds good to me. Talk to you later," said Kay.

After ending the call to her sister, she ran to the bathroom, bent over the commode, and threw up.

"Ann, what is going on with you," Jeff asked as he walked into the bathroom and grabbed a washcloth to wipe Ann's face.

"Hi, honey, I didn't hear you come home," she said as he continued to wipe her face.

"I left early. I wanted to be with you guys," he answered.

"You're going to be so mad at me after you hear what I did today," she sobbed.

"Don't tell me you called that number on the card Lillian sent and talked to her," Jeff sighed while rinsing the washcloth and holding it to Ann's forehead.

"Yes, I did. We met at Roxy's Café and talked for a while this morning," Ann said as she bit her lower lip.

"What did she say," Jeff asked as he led her to the bedroom and helped her lay down on the bed.

"She wants to make some kind of deal with us to pay her a certain amount of money and she will agree to let us keep him," explained Ann.

"I just knew she was trouble. That's why I asked you not to call her," he said firmly.

"I know but there is something else that happened that will raise your anger, too," she said, wondering how Jeff would take the news about what Matthew saw on the playground of the school that day.

"Come on, Ann, quit holding back on me," he insisted.

"Matthew said, while on the playground today, he saw a lady standing across the road staring at him. After asking him to describe what she looked like, it fit perfectly with what Lillian looked like when I met her today," explained Ann. "I called her and she said I better make a deal with her before the court hearing or I would probably lose him in the court hearing. She also threatened me," Ann gasped as she clutched her stomach with a grimace of pain on her face.

"That sounds like she may be hiding something and she is afraid she might not get custody of Matthew. We better call Joe and…"

"I've already called him and made us an appointment to see him at five o'clock this evening. I called Kay and she should be here any minute now," Ann replied.

"I love you so much, Ann. Let's try our level best to try to refrain from getting mad at each other's actions during this horrible ordeal we are going through," he suggested as he embraced his wife.

"I agree with you, Jeff. This has to be the biggest challenge we have encountered since we got married," Ann responded.

"Let's get ready to go," Jeff suggested.

The front doorbell rang, sending Matthew running past their bedroom door.

"Who is this young man here," Kay asked after Matthew opened the door and saw her standing there.

"You know who it is, Aunt Kay," Matthew grinned while running into her open arms.

"I see you're here, Kay," Ann said as she stood next to the door.

"Yeah, I'm ready for a big night babysitting with Matthew…"

"I'm not a baby, Aunt Kay," Matthew interrupted.

"Matthew, your dad and I have to go somewhere this evening and your Aunt Kay is going to stay with you for a while. How does that sound," asked Ann.

"Sounds great to me," he gushed as he grabbed Kay by the hand and led her to the living room.

"Okay, you and Jeff go ahead and get ready to go. I'm sure Matthew and I can find something to do," Kay laughed.

CHAPTER 11

FINDING ANSWERS

The drive to Joe's office was filled with some harsh words being spoken between Jeff and Ann. As Jeff parked the car in front of Joe's law office, Ann was just about ready to explode.

"Now Ann, don't go into Joe's office like a time bomb ready to explode," Jeff said while standing in front of Ann at the door to the office.

"Get out of my way, Jeffery Carl Logan," Ann shouted as she shoved Jeff out of her way before going in the office.

"Good evening, Ann, Jeff. It's good to see you again," Karen said, while noticing the angry looks on Jeff's and Ann's faces. "Joe just finished up with his last client. He said for me to send you two in immediately when you got here. So go on in," Karen said.

"Okay, tell me what's going on now," Joe said as he fumbled through some papers on his desk.

"I met with Lillian Stevens at Roxy's Café earlier today and the way she talked about Matthew, like he was a piece of furniture, made my blood want to boil," Ann said as she tapped her foot on the floor with her arms folded.

"Well, you shouldn't have called her, Ann," Jeff interjected.

"I understand what you're going through," Joe said, trying to calm things down.

"Oh, do you now," Ann sarcastically said. "Have you ever had a child taken away from you?"

"No, I haven't, but I have lost sleep on many cases where I knew deep in my heart that my client deserved to keep the child that was in question about custody and we lost in court. If I hadn't succeeded in other custody cases, I would have walked away from my law firm. I will have you to know that I take medication to help my nerves, because I want to win every case I take on," Joe said as he wiped perspiration from his forehead with his handkerchief.

"I'm sorry how I've acted with you. I'm just feeling so close to having a nervous breakdown, Joe," Ann said.

"Now tell me what you think she is trying to pull," Joe said.

"She wants me to make a deal with her. If we get a settlement in a suit with Hyeres Medical Center, she wants us to give her a certain amount of money then she will let us keep Matthew," Ann said feeling a little more comfortable talking to Joe.

"Did she say how much," Joe asked.

"No, but later on, when Matthew came home from school, he told me about a lady staring at him on the playground today. I asked him to describe her and the description he gave me fit Lillian to a 'T'. I called her and told her to stay away from Matthew. She threatened me and said I could make a deal with her before the court hearing or I would lose Matthew in the court hearing to her," Ann said.

"It sounds like she is trying to hide something and hoping we will not find it before the hearing," Joe said. "I already have a private investigator checking around where she lives. Hopefully when I talk to him this evening, he may have already come up with enough to keep her from getting Matthew due to being an unfit mother," Joe said with a big grin on his face.

"What do we do now, Joe," Jeff asked.

"I will immediately file a motion for continuance with the court. The continuance should be agreeable to both parties in the custody case. I believe we know that this Lillian Stevens will probably not agree to sign it," Joe said.

"What do we do then," Jeff asked.

"The court may decide to hold the hearing at the time scheduled and decide whether to grant the continuance before hearing the rest of the case. In some cases, a judge will have a scheduled telephone conference on the motion for continuance to decide whether to grant it before the scheduled hearing. I will jump on this immediately and see what we can come up with," Joe said, as he picked up the phone and held his hand over the receiver before he whispered, "I can't do much until tomorrow, but I will do what I can this evening," Joe said.

"Thanks so much, Joe, for what you're doing for us," Jeff said as he shook Joe's hand.

"Is this your family," Ann asked as she looked at a big framed picture hanging on the wall behind his desk.

"Yes it is. The little boy you see there in the picture is Joe Junior. He died of congenital heart failure at age five," Joe said with his voice breaking some.

"I'm so sorry for your loss, Joe," Ann said while running her finger along the picture with the little boy in it.

"Thank you. I think it made a more appreciable man out of

me. I used to take on extra cases which left little time with my family. After Joe Junior died, I developed a different perspective on life," said Joe.

"How soon do you think you might know something on the continuance motion," Jeff asked.

"I've got some pretty good connections around town. Hopefully, sometime tomorrow morning," Joe responded.

"I will have a hard time sleeping tonight not knowing if Joe can get that continuance motion filed. We are running out of time," Ann said to Jeff when they walked to the car.

"Let's just hope for the best," Jeff said as they headed back home.

"It looks like you two have been enjoying yourself," Ann said as she watched Kay and Matthew playing an Xbox game on the TV in the living room while they were both laughing out loud.

"This kid is hard to beat," Kay giggled.

"Yeah, I've beat her ten games to one," Matthew laughed.

"Oh no, you won again," Kay said as she laid down the control to the Xbox .

"Kay, it was so good of you to come and stay with Matthew while we went to take care of a business appointment," Ann said.

"You know I would do anything for you except…"

"I know what you're going to say, Kay. Everything except admit I put the frog in your bed late at night when we were kids," Ann giggled.

"Matthew, would you like a bowl of chocolate ice cream," Jeff asked looking at Matthew.

"Sure thing. I would never turn down of bowl of ice cream," he giggled as he followed Jeff into the kitchen.

"So what's up, Ann," Kay asked.

"To make a long story short, a Lillian Stevens, who says she is the mother of Matthew, is trying to make a deal with us before the hearing," Ann said with her voice breaking.

"What kind of deal," Kay asked while raising her eyebrows.

"She thinks we will get a settlement from the Hyeres Medical Center and she offered to let me keep Matthew if I gave her some money," explained Ann.

"Why that greedy..."

"Kay, try not to raise your voice. Matthew may hear you," Ann said looking toward the kitchen and back at Kay. "Our lawyer has someone checking on her to see what kind of mother she is. We are running out of time. The hearing is only two days away and our lawyer is going to try to get a continuance with the court," Ann said

"What is a continuance," Kay asked seeming very confused.

"It means a delay for going to court until our lawyer has time to check her background," Ann responded.

"You keep the family informed on what is going on, Ann," Kay urged. "I need to go tell Matthew bye and head to the grocery store. We are about out of everything."

"Aunt Kay, I heard you say you were leaving. Please stay a while longer," Matthew pleaded as he ran to her in the living room.

"I've got some things to catch up on, Matthew. You be a good boy for your mom and dad," she said while hugging him, grabbing her purse, and heading for the door.

All kinds of scenarios played out in Ann's mind while sleeping during the night. One was so horrific she woke up screaming and pounding on Jeff as she shouted, "I will not let you take him away from me, do you hear me?"

Jeff grabbed her arms to protect himself from the blows she was inflicting upon him. "Ann, wake up, you're having a nightmare. I'm here and Matthew is safely tucked in bed in his bedroom," Jeff said as he held her in his arms until she realized it was only a dream.

"I don't know if I can take much more of Lillian and the chance I might lose custody of Matthew. I have even had dreams of our biological son. When I met with Lillian Stevens, she showed me pictures of James Ray Stevens, the child she had been raising until his death. It really bothered me that she didn't even ask to see pictures of Matthew," Ann sobbed

"We're dealing with a woman who seems to have some mental problems, don't you think," he asked as they fell back on the bed with their pillows propped up behind their heads.

"I think she is weird, crude, and rude and I'm really afraid of her, Jeff," Ann said with her voice breaking on the last word. "Do you mind if I carry that little pistol in my purse that you bought me several years ago to keep here at the house when you are away on business trips?"

"Certainly not, Ann."

"And why not," she snarled.

"Because the last thing in the world we need is you shooting Lillian Stevens and maybe killing her. How do you think Matthew would feel if he knew the woman who has raised him since he was a baby had to go to jail for murder," he asked getting very irritated at the way Ann was acting.

"I'm sorry. You will have to be my rock during all this that is going on with the custody case," she softly said.

"Here, take these pills and maybe that will help prevent you from having an anxiety attack," Jeff said as he held a glass of water and several pills in front of Ann.

"Thanks," said Ann.

The rest of the night was spent by Ann restlessly sleeping and Jeff finding it hard to sleep with Ann mumbling and tossing and turning in bed. Jeff's thoughts were of hoping the next day would be filled with some good news from Joe.

CHAPTER 12

HOPING FOR SOME GOOD NEWS

The sun was lighting up the room and the warmness of it brought Jeff out of bed.

Ann slowly looked at him and mumbled, "Can I have a few more minutes to lie here before I get up to get you and Matthew ready for the day?"

"Yes, that will be fine. I will check with you after I take my shower," he said before heading to the bathroom. Jeff had been trying hard to be that rock Ann could lean on for support, but he felt like it might be such a big challenge that they just might not win.

"You still in bed, mom," Matthew said as he ran into their bedroom and jumped into bed with her.

"Oh Matthew, I have overslept..."

"That's okay, I still have plenty of time to get ready for school and you still have time to fix breakfast. That is according to my atomic watch dad got me last Christmas," he giggled and bounced off the bed before he took off running down the hall to his room.

Sure enough, within a half an hour, Matthew had taken a bath, dressed, eaten his breakfast, and while Ann gathered the dishes off of the table to put everything away, she heard Matthew shout, "See you later, mom."

"Ann, I will call you if I hear anything from Joe today," Jeff said as he kissed her on his way out the door.

The house became so quiet after Matthew and Jeff left, it only left Ann time to sit and think about what might come next. Being so nervous and upset, she began to crave the old habit of smoking. With the insistence of Jeff several years earlier, she quit that foul habit. She grabbed a pair a jeans, a blouse, and shoes. Once she was dressed, she fumbled around in her purse until she found her car keys before she headed for the door. She jumped into her car and closed the door when her cell phone rang, sending her into a panic searching for it in her purse.

"What took you so long to answer my call," the familiar voice of Jeff said.

"I…uh…was cleaning off the breakfast dishes from the table and putting them in the dishwasher. Did Joe call you," Ann asked.

"Yes, he did. Do you want to hear some good news," Jeff teased.

"Yeah, that would be good for a change," Ann responded trying to keep from falling apart.

"Joe called and said we have a continuance and don't have to go to the hearing on July 10th. He also told me that his private investigator has come up with some pretty good information on Lillian Stevens that we can use in the hearing which has been moved to August 12th."

"Oh, that sounds wonderful to me," Ann said while trying to make sense of what he just told her.

79

"Now, you relax some and don't let that pretty little head of yours worry so much," Jeff suggested.

"Okay, I will try my best," she said while biting her lower lip.

"Let me get back to work. I have a ton of things that need doing today. You take care and…"

"And what, Jeff?"

"Remember, I love you very much," he added.

"I feel the same way. Now get to work and I will talk to you later," she said as she ended the call. That helped her nerves enough to stop the cravings for a cigarette, so she decided to go back in the house and catch up on household chores.

Shortly after cleaning up the kitchen, taking a shower, and dressing, she faintly heard her cell phone ringing as she was blow drying her hair. Her stomach began to churn after picking up her cell phone and noticing the name on the caller ID was Lillian. Bracing herself against the bedroom wall, she answered the call.

"Hello, who is this," Ann asked.

"You know who this is," the angry voice of Lillian could be heard. "What kind of bull are you up to now," she shouted so loud that it rang in Ann's ear.

"What do you mean by that, Lillian," Ann asked.

"You know good and well what I mean. My lawyer, Martin Hazelton, just called me and said the hearing was going to be moved to August 12th. Do you think you're going to find something that will keep me from taking that kid away from you? Well, you've got another think coming. You have gone too far now," she shouted sending Ann into an anxiety attack.

Falling to the floor and trembling all over, she dropped the phone, but could still hear Lillian shouting expletives that would make the vilest person cringe. She managed to pick up the phone and softly said, "Why don't you calm down and see if we can work something out."

"I gave you that opportunity and you refused. You are going to fool around and cause me to not only lose that child, but lose any hope of collecting any money from a suit with Hyeres Medical Center. If you really love that kid, you will back off now or I will…"

"You will what, Lillian? You have threatened me once, now you are doing it again. I believe Jeff and I need to call the police and let them handle this because I'm not going to take your verbal abuse anymore," Ann shouted hoping Lillian would back off.

"Let me tell you this. If you call the police, you may get more than you can handle from me," Lillian shouted.

"Yeah, like what would you do," Ann asked.

"That kid may come up missing someday. So be careful what you do, because he could be in harm's way. Now I advise you to back off," snarled Lillian.

"You better….hello…hello?"

Lillian abruptly ended the call.

Ann was in a quandary of what to do. The first question that came to mind was, should she tell Jeff and take the chance they he may, with the help of Joe, push Lillian too far and she may do something terrible, like kill Matthew. The second question was, should she meet with Lillian again and try to pacify her until they could be sure Matthew was safe from harm.

The craving for a cigarette overtook her again after talking to Lillian to the point of running to the car and driving to a little market off Broad Street. She fumbled trying to open the package of cigarettes after purchasing them. After lighting a cigarette, the first big puff of smoke circled around her as she left the market. Finding a bench nearby, she kept taking big puffs off of it trying to calm herself down. Crushing out what was left of the cigarette, she got in her car and drove back home. Totally exhausted, she collapsed in a heap on the sofa in the living room and while sobbing, fell asleep.

Her inherited pendulum clock from her late grandfather that was sitting on the mantle struck the hour of three o'clock waking Ann abruptly from a deep exhausted sleep. Rubbing her eyes and stretching didn't do much for her queasy stomach. After lighting up one of her cigarettes and taking a big puff, she thought about the conversation she had earlier with Lillian. She knew one thing for sure, Lillian was a dangerous person and would make her keep her guard up while dealing with her.

The sound of a school bus stopping in front of the house frightened her with the thought that Matthew would be coming through the front door at any moment. She crushed the half smoked cigarette on a chewing gum paper and stuffed it, along with her pack of cigarettes, in her purse.

Matthew came running in and began sniffing the air. He looked at Ann as she stood in front of him praying he wouldn't be able to recognize the smell of the cigarette she had been smoking.

"What's that smell, Mom," Matthew asked while frowning and holding his nose.

"Uh…I had a candle lit and it was setting on the end table. I decided to blow it out and put it up."

"That's good," said Matthew as he smiled.

"What do you mean by that, young man," Ann teased while giving him a big hug.

"Well, when I go over to my friend Larry's house, his dad smokes cigarettes and what I smelled when I came in today smelled just like that," Matthew said.

"Enough with that. How was school today," Ann asked, trying to change the subject.

"Not much. That lady that had been watching me was found by the principal today wandering down the hall of the school house. I heard several teachers say they found a knife and some kind of plastic strips in her purse," Matthew said as he looked at Ann whose face had lost all color to it.

"Oh Matthew, I'm so glad you are all right…"

"Mom, why are you squeezing me so hard," he asked as Ann tightened her grip on him.

"I'm sorry. How about you run upstairs, do your homework, and clean up for supper. I think there is a super-sized pizza in the freezer if you're interested in having it for supper tonight," she asked.

"Oh yes, that would be good. Can I play one game after I finish my homework," he asked.

"Oh, I guess so," she smiled.

"Great," he shouted as he took off running upstairs.

Ann's hands were trembling as she reached in the freezer for a pizza. With her knees ready to buckle, she lost all consciousness and fell onto the kitchen floor sending the pizza crashing against the wall.

"Ann, Ann, can you hear me? It's Jeff. How are you feeling," he asked as he cradled her in his arms.

"I…I think I'm going to be okay," she answered feeling a little groggy. "I must have passed out."

"Yes, you did Ann. Matthew heard the noise and ran to check on you. He became worried and did the right thing by calling me," Jeff explained to her.

"According to my watch, mom, you were passed out until dad got here and laid you on the sofa. That's about twenty minutes or a little bit more. Are you all right," Matthew asked.

"I believe I'm going to be okay. I guess something must have made me start feeling bad," she lied hoping to keep Matthew from becoming upset. "Now let me find that pizza and get supper fixed," she teased trying to ease the tension in the air.

While eating supper, Matthew was very talkative about what school was like.

"You know Kyle, who is in my math class, said he is adopted and he loves his adoptive parents very much," Matthew said as Ann's eyes widened.

"What have you been telling them at school, young man," Ann demanded.

"I just told some of my friends that there may have been a mix up at the hospital and you all are trying to figure out who I belong to…"

"Matthew," Ann shouted. "You have no right to talk to your friends at school about what is happening right now," she angrily said.

"Ann, don't be so rough on Matthew. It's not his fault that he is going through this right now," Jeff said with a sigh of irritation.

"I'm sorry, Matthew, I just don't want someone to start picking on you. You know bullying is getting out of hand in schools these days," she tenderly said as she looked at him with tears in her eyes.

"Say Matthew, if you have finished eating, how about us going upstairs to your room and playing a game on your Xbox," asked Jeff.

Ann grinned as they took off upstairs. She gathered up the dishes and placed them in the dishwasher as the sound of the house phone began ringing. She immediately ran to the living room and grabbed up the receiver.

"Hello?"

"Ann, this is Joe Richards. May I talk to Jeff, if he is not too busy?"

"Sure. Hold on."

Walking toward the stairs, she shouted, "Jeff, Joe Richards is on the house phone."

Running down the stairs, Jeff said, "We ought to get rid of that old house phone."

"Joe, good to hear from you. What have you found out that you would be calling me this time of evening," Jeff asked.

"My private investigator found out plenty about Lillian Stevens. Would you mind me stopping by for a few minutes so we can go over this, Jeff?"

"No, not at all. We just got through eating and Ann fixed a pie for dessert later on," Jeff said with Ann nodding her head to indicate no in regards to fixing a pie. After a few minutes more of talking to Joe, Jeff hung up the phone.

"I believe you're right about that old house phone, Jeff. I was trying to figure out what was being said. One thing is for sure, I didn't fix any pie for dessert for later on tonight," she said waiting for Jeff to fill her in on what he and Joe talked about on the phone.

"Joe said he had some information to fill us in on about what his private investigator found out concerning Lillian Stevens.

He is coming over here to talk to us about it in twenty minutes. Do you have some kind of pie in the freezer you can heat up," Jeff asked hoping she would say yes.

"I have what was left over from an apple pie Kay brought over last month when she stopped by to show me her new hair style," answered Ann.

"How about seeing if Matthew wants to go over to his friend's house this evening for a while if that is okay with you," Jeff asked. "I will be glad to run him over there before Joe gets here," Jeff suggested, hoping that would get Matthew out of the house while they discussed what Joe had found out from his private investigator.

"That sounds good to me. I will go ask him about it. I'm sure he will be excited about visiting his friend," said Ann as she walked up the stairs. "Well, he is all excited about going to his friend Raymond's house tonight. I called and Evelyn said she would be glad to have Matthew to come over to visit with her son," Ann said when she returned to the living room.

Jeff arrived back at their house after taking Matthew to spend the evening with his friend, Raymond, as Joe pulled up in the driveway.

"Good to see you, Joe. I just dropped Matthew off at one of his friend's house to visit while we talk business," Jeff said while shaking Joe's hand.

"With what I have to tell you about his biological mother, that may be the best idea, Jeff," Joe said as they walked inside the house.

"Joe, good to see you again," Ann said as she handed him a cup of coffee.

"Let's sit in the living room, Joe, and you can get started on telling us what you have found out about Lillian," Jeff suggested.

86

Joe set his laptop down on the coffee table in front of him and with a nervous look on his face, he typed for a few minutes and then looked up at Jeff and Ann. "Margaret Lillian Stevens, who goes by the name Lillian, has a pretty long rap sheet. My private investigator, Gregory Massey, may have found enough on her to show the court that she is an unfit mother and give you legal custody of Matthew."

"You really think so, Joe," Jeff asked.

"Yes I do. I know she has confessed to some of her misdeeds in life but I wanted to see if she had really straightened up her life or fell back into the gutter she was so accustomed to for years. She hasn't changed much. She has made a pretty good living prostituting even while living with Nathaniel Arnold. In fact, Gregory found someone who will be glad to testify how many times he has used her services within the last six months. Now, let me show you some photos of her taken by the escort service for their clientele to look at."

He then pulled up some photos on his laptop of Lillian wearing some revealing clothes and some of her wearing none at all while posing in positions that made Jeff and Ann immediately look the other way. Before he could continue, Ann placed her hand over her mouth, jumped up, and took off running toward the hallway.

"Can you excuse me a minute or two, Joe," Jeff asked before running down the hall as he heard Ann throwing up in the bathroom.

"Ann, are you all right," Jeff asked as he grabbed a washcloth. He ran cool water onto it and began wiping her face. "Do you not want to go through what Joe has found out? Would you like me to go over it with Joe and then tell you what he found out," Jeff asked becoming very concerned with how upset Ann had become.

"No, I want to see and know everything, too. Let's go back

in the living room and let Joe continue with what he has found out about her," Ann said as she looked in the mirror and straightened her hair.

"I'm so sorry, Ann," Joe said as he looked at Ann with tears welled up in her eyes.

"I want to hear what you found out so far, but it makes me sick to think a despicable person like her may take Matthew away from me with some underhanded scheme of hers," she said with her voice cracking.

"She's not going to do that if I have anything to do with it. I promise you I will work day and night, if necessary, to make sure we have enough information on her to keep her from taking the child you have been raising," Joe declared, while giving her time to compose herself so they could continue.

"Here is one of your anxiety pills, Ann," Jeff said while handing her a pill with a glass of water.

"Thanks," Ann mumbled before swallowing the pill and chasing it down with the glass of water.

"Do you want me to wait a few minutes until you settle your nerves some, Ann," Joe asked.

"No, please continue," Ann said as Jeff held her hand.

"Contrary to what that letter she sent to you says, she continued her evil ways after moving in with Nathaniel. He was fine with that, because it helped pay the bills and allowed them to buy a real nice car."

"What did she do with James Ray Stevens, the child she was raising who was our biological child, while she partied most of the night? Did Nathaniel keep him most of the time while she worked the streets," Ann asked as she tried to keep from falling apart. "Oh, maybe I'm asking too much," Ann said taking a deep breath and waiting for a reply from Joe.

"My private investigator digs deep when I assign him to investigate someone. Gregory said she and Nathaniel would leave him at some friend's house or sometimes she would take him along and ask to leave him in another room while she bedded a client from the escort service she worked for. I..,"

Ann was getting very flustered and interrupted, "That woman must have ice water in her veins? I don't think she has a compassionate bone in her miserable body."

"I believe we have enough on her for the court to find her unfit to raise a child," Joe said with a confident look on his face.

"Are you really sure you can pull this off, Joe," Ann asked with tears in her eyes.

"Of all the cases I've handled like this, I think this will be a slam dunk for sure," he said with a big grin on his face. "Now, if there are no more questions, I'll take that piece of pie that was offered to me by Jeff and a hot cup of coffee," he laughed as Ann got up and headed for the kitchen.

After she left the room, Joe moved a little closer to Jeff and softly said, "You must try to convince Ann that worrying about the outcome of the hearing is not going to help her."

"I know, but you know that Lillian has made threats on Ann's life, and who knows what she may try to do before the hearing," Jeff responded.

"Yes, I understand. Please tell her to be careful..."

"Careful about what," Ann asked while carrying a tray into the living room with coffee and slices of pie on it.

"Just advising Jeff to make sure you are careful with all you do until the hearing. Keep the doors locked. Do you have security on the house," asked Joe.

"Yes we do," Jeff nodded.

"Fine. Keep it set and watch out for Lillian or someone she may pay to…"

"Go ahead and say it, Joe. Keep a watch out for Lillian or someone she may pay to kill me," Ann snarled trying to keep from shouting at Joe in frustration.

"Yes, that's what I wanted to say. I will keep you all informed of anything pertinent to the case and will meet with you a day prior to the hearing. Say, this pie is delicious," Joe said as he ate the last bit of pie on his plate.

"Would you like another piece, Joe?"

"No, I need to run some errands for my wife before I go home. I will keep in touch with you. Have a good night," Joe said as he gathered up his laptop and headed for the door.

"I'll go pick up Matthew from his friend's house, Ann, if that is okay with you," Jeff asked while waiting for a reply from her.

"Yes, yes, Jeff. Please do," she answered with a dazed look on her face.

"Are you all right, Ann," Jeff asked, now holding her hands and looking into her eyes.

"Yes. I'm all right. Go on and pick up Matthew. It is way past his bedtime," Ann said.

After Jeff left, she began gathering up the cups and plates in the living room. She set them on the tray and walked toward the kitchen as her cell phone rang.

She nearly dropped the tray. She quickly set it on the kitchen table and grabbed up her phone. All she heard was silence. She then picked up the tray and placed the cups and dishes in the dishwasher. After closing the door and turning it on, her cell phone rang again. Once again, all she heard was silence on her phone.

She hurried to make sure the security was set and walked to her bedroom to take a relaxing bath. After stepping in the bath tub, she heard a thump that sounded like it came from the front porch. She wrapped a robe around her body and slowly walked toward the door. Looking out and seeing no one in the shadows, she started to turn around and head back to the bedroom to take her bath when she took a second look. A dusty set of foot prints could be seen on the front porch. A chill ran down her spine as she ran to the kitchen and grabbed one of her big steak knives. She slowly walked over to the front window and pulled back the curtain a few inches where she began looking through the darkness to see if someone like Lillian might be stalking her. She thought if she turned on the porch light, if someone was stalking her, they might run and she would not be able to see who it was. A few minutes passed, the pill kicked in, and with her energy drained, she fell asleep on the sofa.

"Ann, Ann," Jeff said as he finds her asleep on the sofa.

Abruptly waking up she became confused and started swinging the steak knife at Jeff. He managed to get it out of her hand as Matthew looked at her with a terrified look on his face.

Laying the knife down on the coffee table, Jeff took her into his arms and began hugging her. "What in the world made you so frightened that you would be asleep on the sofa in your robe with a steak knife in your hand," Jeff asked.

"Yeah mom, what in the world scared you so," Matthew asked as he sat beside her.

"I was getting into the bath tub to take a bath when I heard a thump that sounded like it was coming from the front porch. Looking out, I didn't see anyone, but before I turned around to go back to the bedroom, I took a second look and saw what looked like footprints on the front porch," Ann sobbed.

"I'll go check it out," Jeff said as he headed for the front door. A few minutes later he walked back into the living room with a grim look on his face. "You were right, there are some footprints but it could have been the mail carrier who left them when he delivered the mail today," Jeff offered, trying to calm her down.

"Not on the left side of the porch next to the big window, Jeff. You know as well as I do that the mail box is on the opposite side of the door from where the footprints I saw tonight are. There has not been any rain lately and the dust from footsteps during the day are usually blown off by the wind," she said with her voice cracking.

"Okay, Ann, I will give you the benefit of the doubt. Just don't go out and check on something like that at night. If I'm not around, call the police," Jeff sternly said.

"I will," she said sadly.

"Let's all get ready for bed. What do you say about that. Matthew," Jeff asked as he grabbed Matthew up like a sack of potatoes and started walking toward the stairs while Mathew giggled.

Once they settled down for the night, Ann found it hard to close her eyes. After tossing and turning for several hours, she drifted off to sleep. Just about daybreak, she raised up in the bed and shouted, "Don't kill me, Lillian!"

"Ann, you're having a bad dream. Wake up," Jeff said while grabbing her by the arms and trying to calm her down.

"I'm sorry. I had a dream that Lillian broke into the house and was standing at the end of the bed with a large knife and a scary look on her face," said Ann.

"Well, she's not here, Ann. You need to settle down and get some sleep so you can keep a clear head for what we will have to face in the hearing," Jeff softly said.

"I will try," she replied while laying back down. Sleep was hard to come by for her the rest of the night.

CHAPTER 13

HOW QUICKLY THINGS CHANGE

The next morning, the alarm went off on Jeff's cell phone that startled Ann upon hearing it.

Jeff bent down by the side of the bed and whispered to Ann, "You rest a few more minutes. I have some work I need to get a head start on at the office. I'll grab something to eat from the break room later on."

Ann grinned at him with a groggy feeling due to lack of sleep. When he left, she drifted off to sleep. After having one frightening dream after another, she rubbed her eyes, stretched out her arms, and managed to make her way to the shower. She quickly dressed, walked into Matthew's room, and before waking him up, she took a long look at him lying on his bed with a peaceful look on his face.

"Time to get up, Matthew," she softly said.

"Why not let me skip a day from school," he asked with a slight grin on his face.

"You know I'm not going to let you do that. Go take a

shower and get dressed for school.   I will have some pancakes and chocolate milk ready for you," she said as she watched him slowly make his way to the bathroom.

After making the pancakes and pouring chocolate milk, a loud thumping sound could be heard. With her hand shaking, she grabbed a large steak knife from a drawer in the kitchen and slowly walked toward the front door.

"Mom, what was that sound," Matthew asked as he came bounding down the stairs and into the living room.

Ann placed her hand to her mouth indicating to Matthew to be quiet. She slowly opened the door and looked outside to see if she could figure out what could have made the sound they heard.

Before she could open the door any further, she felt something hard hit the hand that held the knife. It went flying across the porch as a very scary looking Lillian stood in front of her.

"All right, you and the boy are going to take a ride with me," Lillian said as she held a knife against Ann's throat.

"Please don't kill my mom," Matthew shouted and started kicking Lillian's legs.

"Tell him to back off or I will cut your throat right here," Lillian angrily shouted.

"Matthew, please quit kicking her legs or she will cut my throat," Ann shouted as some blood trickled down from her neck where Lillian had been pressing the knife against her throat.

"Now turn around and let me tie your hands together," Lillian shouted as Ann reluctantly turned around. "Now, tell the boy…"

"He has a name, Lillian. I wish you would use it," Ann said while tears rolled down her cheeks.

"He is my son and I'll worry about that later on…"

"Where are you taking us," Ann cried out.

"I'm not dumb enough to tell you where that is," Lillian said as she finished tying Ann's hands behind her back. "Let me go get that son of mine. He is my meal ticket out of this country."

"Why do you want to do this, Lillian? There is no doubt you should get a good bit of money from the Hyeres Medical Center for the mix up of our boys," Ann pleaded.

"Don't you move, I'm going to go find the boy and tie him up and we will be out of here," Lillian angrily said as she walked into the house leaving Ann alone on the front porch.

Within moments, Ann heard Matthew screaming at the top of his lungs, "Don't kill my mom!"

Ann started to walk back into the house when all of a sudden, she saw Lillian dragging Matthew toward the front door.

"We have to get out of here in a hurry. This little brat called the cops before I could find him. Let's get in my car now," Lillian shouted as she pushed Ann and Matthew toward her car. Before cramming them into the back seat of the car, she wrapped and covered their eyes with some pieces of cloth and shoved them into her car. Within minutes, Ann could sense they were traveling at a high rate of speed.

"The cops will catch up with you and then what are you going to do," Matthew's muffled voice could be heard from the cramped position in the floor board of the back seat.

"You better keep him quiet if you all want to breathe another breath of life," Lillian shouted as she jerked the wheel to keep from hitting a car that pulled out in front of her.

All kinds of scenarios played out in Ann's mind as Lillian sped down the streets, turning sharply from one street to another slamming Ann and Matthew from one side of the car to the other. After what seemed like an hour or two, she could hear the sound of the car being driven inside of a building.

"Did you have any trouble getting them here, Lillian," a dull sounding voice could be heard next to the car.

"Nah, I showed them who was boss pretty quickly," said Lillian. "Got a cigarette?"

"Yeah, here, have a pack while I grab them and lock them in the back," the dull sounding voice was heard by Ann and Matthew sending chills down her back and made Matthew whimper. After stumbling along for a good distance, a big rusty sounding door could be heard by Ann and Matthew. Within a few minutes, the blindfolds and the plastic ties that Lillian had used to tie their hands were removed.

Ann blinked several times trying to adjust her eyes to the dimly lit room. A pungent smell filled her nostrils and made her stomach churn.

"Just call me Jed for now," a heavy set man dressed in a well-worn suit said as he looked through eye holes in a dingy hood on his head. "Just make yourself at home," he joked and quickly walked out of the room and the sound of the door closing made Ann become very nervous.

Matthew cried out," Mom, are they going to kill us now?"

Ann wrapped her arms around him. "Not if I have anything to do with it," Ann softly said trying not to sound too frightened. Looking around the room, she was able to make out some faded words on one of the walls. To her, it looked like it spelled out Hodge Warehouse. With a lump in her throat she thought, *what a lousy place to die.*

The hours seemed to pass so slowly and the room became very cold sending Ann looking for something to cover them with. After looking around the room, she spotted several old burlap sacks and wrapped them around Matthew and her. The light that was coming through a dingy window in the top wall of the building began to dim until darkness filled the room and the chill made them shake forcing their teeth to chatter as they clung together.

CHAPTER 14

I WAS HOPING IT WAS A DREAM

Ann awoke with a start.

"When?... What?... Wh...," she mumbled.

"You're here with me, mom," said Matthew as he, too, awoke from a doze.

"Aww-gee, I was hoping it was a dream," Ann said with disappointment coloring her voice and the shakes from the damp chilly air.

"I'm scared," whimpered Matthew.

"Me, too," Ann replied as she looked around to scope everything out again.

Ann stood up, slowly, forcing her body to move from its position on the floor. Everything ached. She must have laid in one position for too long.

With a great deal of effort, she forced herself to walk around what seemed to be a concrete and metal warehouse.

She could see only one set of doors and when she pushed

on them, she discovered they were locked, probably with a padlock from the outside.

A couple of windows high up from the floor allowed some light to filter into the gigantic room. There was barely enough light to walk around without tripping on something and causing bodily harm.

"Mom, I have to go pee," said Matthew as he clutched himself to emphasize his point.

"Walk over to that corner," Ann said. "I'll go with you to check it out and then walk away to give you some privacy."

"Isn't there a bathroom," asked Matthew.

"I don't see one. Come on, we'll check out the corner. When you're finished, I will have to go pee, too," said Ann as she nudged him to get him moving.

When all of the call of nature duties were taken care of, they both surveyed the huge warehouse again and again. They walked to every place that could be easily seen until exhaustion overcame them and they had to sit on the cold damp concrete covered with the smelly burlap sacks.

Nothing like this had ever happened to Ann. She had no idea how she was going to get them both out of this mess but she knew she had to do it. She could no longer rely on the comfort of the sedatives to calm her so her husband could take care of the situation. He was not there to take over. She had to do it herself.

She had seen an old rickety ladder in the far corner, but that would not do any good because it was not long enough to reach the high windows. Even if it were long enough, how would she be able to climb down from the other side? The windows appeared to be up high like a second or third story but, because it was a warehouse, there was no second or third story.

Her belly started rumbling and she realized she was hungry.

99

She had no idea what time it was except that it was daylight as shown from the windows.

Her arm was hurting and when she rubbed it, she felt a sore spot that hadn't been there previously. Slowly she traced her finger over the area and realized she had been injected with something that was probably the reason she had fallen asleep.

She glanced at Matthew and saw that he had dozed off again. She wanted to check him for an injection site but decided it could wait. She wanted him to sleep as much as possible through this ordeal. It wouldn't be so hard on him if he slept through it.

She extricated herself from Matthew's arms and started walking again. She needed to find a way out of this warehouse. There had to be another exit somewhere.

She walked further into the opposite end of the building where it was much darker. There didn't seem to be any windows to allow the little bit of light to sneak inside.

"I wish I had a flashlight," Ann mumbled as she tried to see what was stored, if anything, in the dark end of the building.

She held her arms outstretched in front of her body and walked slowly, sliding her feet along the concrete so she wouldn't trip over something she couldn't see.

She heard something.

Keys rattled against metal. Someone was trying to get the padlock to open.

Ann ran as fast as she dared to get back to Matthew before the door opened. She threw herself down on the floor next to her son and pulled the burlap sacks up and over both of their bodies as she willed herself to breathe slower.

"Mom," said Matthew softly.

"Sh-sh-sh," shushed Ann as she held her finger up to her lips. "Someone's coming inside."

Ann felt Matthew's body stiffen from fright. She knew her own body was tense and ready to spring.

CHAPTER 15

ANN IS MISSING

Jeff called the house several times without an answer. He was getting irritated with the constant ringing and no pick up. He tried Ann's cell phone but it was not activated. She would do that occasionally; forget to turn it on, until she noticed it when she picked it up to go somewhere.

"Ann? Are you here," shouted Jeff as soon as he opened the front door. He had no idea why Ann had left the door unlocked. She knew better than that especially since there was a crazy woman running around trying to do her harm.

Who knew what Lillian would do?

Jeff walked into the kitchen and spotted Ann's cell phone laying on the counter; her handbag was sitting next to it.

He ran up the stairs to their bedroom but it was also empty. After checking out Matthew's bedroom, he raced back down the stairs and found Matthew's school backpack tossed on the sofa.

"What is happening," he said as he ran his hands through his hair in frustration.

He ran out the front door and looked around the place front

and back until he satisfied himself that Ann was nowhere to be found.

He knocked on the neighbor's door on the right side of his house.

"Mary, have you seen Ann today," he asked as he pushed his hands through his hair again.

"No, Jeff, I haven't seen her but I just arrived home a few minutes ago. I'm sorry," she said as she started to close her door.

"Thanks," he mumbled as he walked away to cross his yard and visit the neighbor on the other side of his house.

He knocked and rang the doorbell but there was no answer.

He glanced at the house across the street. The inhabitants were new in the neighborhood and weren't very friendly. As a matter of fact, he had never actually met his new neighbors.

With a great deal of reluctance, he walked across the street, up the sidewalk, and pounded on the front door. Normally, he would have knocked firmly and not pounded, but the noise echoing from the interior of the house prompted him to pound and pound very hard.

He stood for a couple of minutes without anyone appearing at the doorway. He pounded again and again until his hands were getting tender and sore from the abuse.

"Hey! What do you want," asked a scruffy man with a rag tied around his head and another rag of contrasting color and bold print tied around his neck.

"I'm Jeff Logan, your neighbor from across the street. I need to ask you an important question," he explained with apprehension. He sensed that something wasn't right but he couldn't put his finger on the problem

"Okay, get on with it," snapped the scruffy man as he shouted over the so-called music coming from behind him.

"Like I said, I live across the street and I was wondering if you might have seen my wife, Ann, leave and with whom," asked Jeff knowing he wasn't going to get the answer he needed to hear.

"I ain't got time to watch the neighbors," growled the stranger as he backed away to make enough room to close the door.

"Please, my wife is missing and there may be some foul play involved," said Jeff sternly.

"Not my problem, I got to get back to work now," snarled the stranger.

"Before I leave, can you tell me your name," asked Jeff as he tried to curtail his anger.

"John Smith," the stranger said as he slammed the door.

"That was a colossal waste of time," Jeff mumbled as he turned on his heel to walk back across the street.

He re-entered his house and looked around again. When he had satisfied his need to double check, to make sure that he needed help, he placed an emergency call to his lawyer, Joe Richards.

"Joe, Ann is missing," said Jeff excitedly.

"What?"

"Ann is missing. I think that Lillian Stevens woman has taken Ann and Matthew," he said as his voice rose in volume.

"Are you sure," asked Joe.

"She is nowhere to be found. Her handbag is here along with her cell phone. Matthew's backpack is still here but I haven't called the school yet. I'll do that when I hang up from talking with you," he explained breathlessly as he fought the urge to scream.

"Have you checked all the neighbors," questioned Joe.

"Of course, I'm not stupid. Ann is missing and I think Matthew is with her. What should I do," sputtered Jeff.

"Nothing. Stay right there. I'll be there in a few minutes," Joe said as he tried to help his client and friend.

CHAPTER 16

THEY ARE GONE

Jeff paced.

He made himself stop pacing when he realized he could be destroying evidence. He walked to the front door, exited the house, and sat on the porch steps awaiting the arrival of Joe Richards.

"Joe will know what I should do," he mumbled as he ran his hands through his hair in frustration.

Sitting was not helping Jeff. He had to get up and move. He walked to the street, turned, and returned to the steps not looking at anything in particular. He kept his head down on his next trip up and down the sidewalk. That's when he spotted them.

Ann's keys were laying on the ground wedged up against the edge of the sidewalk almost hidden from sight.

He did not move them. He didn't pick them up because he wanted to show Joe exactly where they were and what it meant to find them there.

He walked on to see if he could find something else; some hint of what happened to Ann and Matthew.

106

"Matthew? Oh God, I forgot to call the school," he said loudly to no one at all.

Jeff ran back inside the house to find the phone number for Matthew's school.

"Hello," he said when a very polite young lady answered the ring. "I need to find out if Matthew Logan is present in school today. I found his backpack at home and I was worried about him," he explained, hoping they would give him an answer.

"One moment, please," she said as she silenced the call.

The line opened and the young lady asked, "Who are you?"

"I'm sorry. I'm Jeff Logan, Matthew's father," he answered. "It's really important for me to know if he made it to school. His mother, Ann, is missing and I think Matthew may be with her. So, please tell me if he showed up at school," he pleaded.

"No sir. He is absent today. Is there anything else I can do for you," she asked politely.

"No, I think not. Hopefully, I will have him back in school tomorrow. Thank you for talking with me," Jeff said as he disconnected the call.

He sat on the barstool next to the counter in the kitchen and stared into space.

A car horn started blaring in front of his house. The noise brought him back to reality and the need to go meet Joe to let him inside the house popped into his head. Jeff needed all of the help he could get to find his missing family.

"Joe, they are gone. I think that crazy woman has taken them," said Jeff excitedly.

"How do you know that, Jeff? Has anyone called you?

107

Did you receive a written demand, or a text, or an email," Joe asked as he tried to gather as much information as he could get from Jeff who was rapidly dissolving into a helpless mass of male.

"No, well, I don't think so. I haven't checked my smart phone for anything. It hasn't made a sound so I never thought about it," said Jeff as he went in search of his cell phone that he had laid down somewhere when he entered the house.

He found it in the living room on the coffee table where he had placed it when he found Matthew's school backpack.

The light in the front on the upper right hand corner was blinking indicating something had been transmitted to his phone.

He grabbed for the phone and pressed the button to light up the screen where the icons in the upper left hand corner would tell him where he should look.

The array of icons ran across the top indicating he had some Yahoo mail messages, some G-mail, a text, a voice message, and a missed phone call. When the cell phone started vibrating as he held it, he realized that he must have turned off the sound earlier in the day.

He rapidly punched buttons that would allow him to answer the incoming call.

"Hello," he screamed to the poor person on the other end,

"Hello? Mr. Logan?"

"Yes, this is Jeff Logan," he said apologetically.

"Is Mr. Richards there with you," the female voice asked meekly.

"Joe, this call is for you," he said as he handed the cell phone to Joe.

"Mr. Richards, this is Karen. You just had a peculiar phone

call from a man who was disguising his voice. He said if you want to ever see Ann Logan and Matthew Logan again to gather up five hundred thousand dollars, unmarked, no dye packs, in twenties and fifties, and place them in a metal briefcase. What do you want me to do, Mr. Richards," Karen asked apprehensively.

"Just keep your notes. Did you take a look at the number that showed up on the caller I.D.," Joe asked Karen.

"Yes sir, I did but it was marked "Private".

"Okay, Karen. I will be here with Jeff Logan for a while. The police may come and question you about the phone message because I'm going to call them as soon as I get off this call."

"Yes sir," said Karen as she disconnected the line.

"Jeff, did you call the police," asked Joe.

"No, I was waiting for you to get here. I really didn't know what to tell them except that Ann and Matthew aren't where they are supposed to be," he explained.

"Well, now you can tell them they have been kidnapped and they are asking for a ransom of five hundred thousand dollars," said Joe as he watched Jeff's face drain of color.

"Five hundred thousand dollars? I don't have that kind of money," he sputtered.

"The kidnapper seems to think that you do," said Joe.

"I don't know why. If it's that Lillian Stevens woman, she knows we don't have any money. She also knows that we might receive a hefty settlement because of the hospital's blunder," he said knowing that Joe already knew about the problem of Matthew's exchange at birth.

"What am I going to do, Joe? How am I going to get my family back safe and sound," asked Jeff not even trying to hide the desperation.

"We need to call the police, right now. They can give us a hand with solving this problem," said Joe with all the encouragement he could muster.

Joe pulled his cell phone from his pocket and started punching in numbers.

"Who are you calling? It certainly isn't 9-1-1," said Jeff as he watched Joe.

"I called a detective friend of mine. I think he would be the best person to help us with this problem," explained Joe.

"I hope so," mumbled Jeff as he ran his fingers through his hair showing his frustration.

CHAPTER 17

DO YOU HAVE ANY ENEMIES?

Jeff showed Joe where Ann's keys were laying and pointed out that she did not have her handbag or cell phone with her. Also, Matthew's school backpack was still on the sofa so Joe saw that, too.

Sirens could be heard as they were getting closer to the house.

"I hope they can help me," said Jeff as he sat on a barstool next to the kitchen counter. He lowered his head onto his hands with his arms propped up on his elbows.

"Jeff Logan, this is Detective Dennis White. He has handled cases like this so he knows what has to be done," said Joe.

"Nice to meet you, Detective White. I do hope you can help me get my family home," said Jeff.

"I'll do my best, Mr. Logan. I do need you to show me everything and then I will ask you some questions," said Detective White.

Jeff started his explanation of details to the detective with the fact that Ann had not answered her cell phone when he called

111

several times. When he arrived home, he found the handbag and cell phone so he knew there was a problem. Then he saw the school backpack. When he was walking around outside, he spotted Ann's keys on the ground. He called Joe because he didn't know what else to do.

"When did you find out that they had been taken," asked Detective White.

"When Joe Richards, my lawyer, told me he had received a ransom call saying they wanted five hundred thousand dollars," answered Jeff.

"You've never actually talked to them," said the detective.

"No sir, I have not," Jeff answered. "You'll have to ask Joe about the call. He didn't actually receive the call. His secretary called him with the ransom information."

"Do you have any enemies," asked Detective White.

"Only one that I am aware of. Her name is Lillian Stevens. She is trying to take my son away from me through the courts," Jeff said bitterly.

"How is she planning to do that," asked the detective.

"It's a long story, Detective White," said Jeff.

"Let's hear it," demanded the detective.

Jeff explained the baby switching event up to present day to the detective in as few words as possible. He wanted the detective to do something about finding his family and talking to him endlessly didn't seem to be what Jeff wanted to do.

Once Jeff had finished his explanation, the detective asked, "Are you sure you have no other enemies?"

"None that I am aware of," snapped Jeff as his anger was definitely growing.

"When is the court hearing scheduled," asked the detective.

"Next week; actually Monday and that is only four days from today. Of course, the whole thing may be moot if we don't find my family. She will have won without going to court. What I hear from other people I have talked with is that our chance of winning the legal action is next to nothing because Lillian Stevens is the biological mother. The courts lean heavily toward that end. It would be such an unjust decision by an unjust court if that happens. We have raised Matthew as our son. He is our son. No court can take him away from us," stammered Jeff. "Please find them for me. Or, if you can't find them, I will look for them myself."

"Mr. Logan, it is our job and we will do everything possible to find your family to return them to you unharmed," said Detective White in the tone of a man who had repeated those words on several occasions. They were flat and lacked conviction as far as Jeff was concerned.

"When do you plan to start," demanded Jeff.

"What do you mean," asked the detective.

"When do you plan to stop talking to me and start looking," snapped Jeff.

"As soon as we get all of the information we need such as where to begin looking. You've got to understand, Mr. Logan, that we are newcomers to this problem. You know everything that has happened but we can only interpret the circumstances through what you tell us. If you distort the truth or lie to us in any way, it will lead us down the wrong path," said the even toned detective as he tried to calm Jeff's anger and fear.

"I've told you everything, Detective White," said Jeff solemnly.

"You need to leave this to us. We will find her and your son. You need to stay here in case they contact you. You certainly don't want to miss the call, do you," asked Detective White.

"No, I don't."

Detective White turned on his heels and walked away to talk to a couple of uniformed officers standing just inside the door.

Jeff couldn't hear the exchange of words. He really didn't want to hear them because he knew they were at a loss as to where to locate his family until they could uncover some further information through whatever computer searches they needed to complete.

In the meantime, as soon as the coast was clear, he would do some searching himself on the computer and everywhere else he could think of. He was going to find his family, with or without the help of Detective White and his entourage.

"Mr. Logan, we have a trap and trace set up on your phone line and we don't feel it is necessary to tie up a man sitting here in the house with you. We don't feel that you are in any danger. What do you think, sir," asked Detective White.

"I agree with you. I don't need a baby-sitter because I'm not the one in danger. It's my wife and son who are in danger. Use as many men as possible to find them, please," begged Jeff.

"Yes sir," said Detective White as he instructed his men to load up and return to the station to get further instructions.

As soon as all of the legal personnel had left his home, he walked to the telephone and dialed the necessary numbers for call forwarding to his cell phone. He wasn't going to miss the phone call; if one was made to him. But he wasn't going to sit around and wait for it either.

CHAPTER 18

THE POLICE POKED AND PRODDED

Finally, the police left the Logan house after having poked and prodded into any area they thought might be of value in finding Ann and Matthew.

Jeff had signed a form allowing them to put a trace on his house telephone line, but he couldn't figure out how that could help because the ransom call had been made to his attorney's office, not his home. But who knows, maybe they will call him at home the next time.

The detective instructed him to try to gather the money, some money, if he couldn't get the whole five hundred thousand. In case he was being watched, Jeff had to be seen working on getting the funds together to pay off the ransom.

Jeff did exactly as instructed. He gathered as much ready cash as he could from several different accounts but came up terribly short of the required five hundred thousand dollars. His only avenue left for getting the remaining cash, if push came to shove, was to borrow it and he wasn't sure a bank, any bank, would loan him that kind of money to pay a ransom.

Joe Richards had returned to his office to await further instructions from the kidnappers, at which time, he would call Detective White and relay the information to him.

That left Jeff with the hardest job. He had to wait. Jeff wasn't good at waiting.

Sitting around the house waiting for some kind of answer whether it was from the police or his lawyer, just wasn't going to happen. He had to get out and look for his family.

Jeff grabbed a bologna sandwich and made himself a strong cup of coffee. He was beginning to feel hungry and didn't want the need to eat to keep him from looking for Ann and Matthew. Besides, he needed for a little bit of time to pass since their leaving, just in case they were to check up on him.

Jeff watched out his front window as he chewed on his sandwich.

"No sign of the police," he whispered.

He continued to pace and chew until the sandwich was eaten, the coffee was swallowed, and his patience was ended.

He walked out to his car glancing about looking for signs of the legal authorities. He climbed into his car, glancing out his rearview mirror and both side mirrors. He started the engine and sat there trying to figure out his next step.

"What is my next step? Where do I look? I have no idea where to start," Jeff said as he broke down into fierce sobs. He sobbed until he was completely drained.

Jeff glanced up at his rearview mirror again, checking for the police, when he caught a glimpse of his neighbor from across the street peering out his window.

He sat in the car watching his neighbor watching him.

"What is that all about," he mumbled as he started his engine. He glanced again at his rearview mirror and the neighbor's face was still plastered to the window with only his eyes moving.

Jeff backed out of the driveway without any idea of where he was going. He just needed to be looking but first he was going to go around the block to see if the neighbor's face was hanging in the front window when he returned.

He drove slowly back to his house just in time to see a figure run around to the back, probably to the patio door.

He didn't pull into his driveway. Instead, he drove right onto his neighbor's driveway that lived to the right of his house. They were not usually home at this time of the day so he knew he wouldn't have a problem with parking there and strolling to the back yard to look into his own patio. He exited his car slowly, not slamming the door, and sneaked around the back of his neighbor's house.

The window in the door is broken and he must still be in there, thought Jeff as he reached for the cell phone that was in his pocket.

Suddenly, before he could get 9-1-1 punched into his cell phone, he saw his neighbor burst through the door carrying two bags and what looked like his computer.

"Hey! Stop," Jeff shouted as he took off running toward his patio.

Jeff ran past the broken door and on around the house to get to the front so he could see his neighbor head off across the street.

That didn't happen. He totally lost sight of his neighbor who seemed to have disappeared into thin air.

Maybe I'm wrong. Maybe it isn't my neighbor, thought Jeff as he walked back to his car where he did complete his 9-1-1 call to summon the police to return and investigate the intrusion.

CHAPTER 19

WAITING FOR INSTRUCTIONS

Ann watched the door as she waited for it to open and her captor to enter. She held onto Matthew for fear that whoever was doing this to them would snatch him away from her.

The door opened slowly and two bags were placed inside before the body could be seen. When he did appear, he was carrying a computer.

"I brought you some fresh clothes if you want to change. I also brought the computer for the boy to play on. There is no access to the Internet so don't think you can call for help," he said with a laugh.

"How long are you going to keep us here in the warehouse," Ann said harshly.

"Don't know yet," he snapped.

"Why don't you know," Ann demanded.

"Waiting for instructions," he snarled.

"From whom," Ann screamed.

"The boss," he yelled in return.

"What does the boss want," Ann asked in a little softer tone.

"For you to shut up, lady," he said as he walked toward the door.

"What do you want," Ann asked in a loud, harsh whisper.

The man with the scraggily hair, unshaven face with earrings and studs in places unimaginable highlighting skin covering tattoos, answered with a grunt.

"Tell me what you want," Ann continued a little louder.

"The boy," he said in a tone that silenced Ann for a moment.

"What are you going to do to us," she pleaded.

The man handed her a third, smaller bag.

"What's this," Ann asked.

"Food," he snarled as he pulled a carton of milk from his pocket and handed her a cup of black coffee with packets of creamer and sugar.

"Eat," he said loudly.

The door slammed and the lock snapped loudly as it was closed.

Ann grabbed the bags of clothes and food and moved them to the area where they had made their bed. She handed Matthew the computer, a sandwich, and the milk.

"Eat, honey, then we will figure out how to get out of here," she whispered.

Ann sipped at her coffee as she pondered her problem. Her

gaze jumped from corner to corner of the huge room searching for a way out into the world of sane people and away from the crazy ones that were holding the two of them hostage.

"Mom, when can we go home," asked Matthew.

"Soon, baby, real soon. Have you turned on the computer," Ann asked.

"Yeah, I'm letting it warm up a bit," he answered.

"See what you can do on that thing, Maybe you can get a message out," said Ann.

"I'll try but I don't think there is any wi-fi," said Matthew.

"You work on that and I'll keep scouting around. There has got to be another way out of here," whispered Ann conspiratorially.

The corner in the darkest part of the building was drawing Ann's attention. There were boxes and fifty gallon drums pushed up against the far side of the building hiding the wall completely.

"Matthew, I'm going to walk over to that corner," Ann said as she pointed. "I'm going to find out what's behind those boxes. You keep working with the computer. Okay?"

"Okay," Matthew answered as he focused on the computer screen.

Ann carried her coffee cup and walked to the dark corner.

"What I wouldn't give for a good flashlight," she mumbled as she inched further into the darkness.

The boxes were big and filled with merchandise. She couldn't read the words on the side of each box due to the darkness so she had no idea what she was planning to shove out of her way.

She reached up to try to grab hold of the box on the top to pull it forward and off of the one setting directly beneath it. The bottom box came to her chest, so the box on the top was well above her.

She worked her way as close as she could get to the box, stretched out her arms, and tried to encircle the big box. That didn't work. The box was too big for her to grab hold with a good grip besides the fact that the box at the side of it was stacked too close.

She stepped back to try to figure out what to do next.

She felt a slight puff of air blowing against her legs.

"There has to be a door behind those boxes," she mumbled. "But how can I move them?"

"Mom, come here a second, please," shouted Matthew.

Ann walked back to the sleeping area.

"What," asked Ann as she leaned over Matthew's shoulder to look at the computer screen.

Matthew had placed the computer on an overturned fifty gallon drum and was using on old wooden folding chair that had been propped up against the wall next to the door.

"Someone other than you, dad, or me has been using this computer," he said accusingly.

"How can you tell," Ann asked with a spark of interest.

"There is a file on here with a strange name. I've not seen it before today. Do you remember naming a file JR and MLS," asked Matthew.

"No, I didn't. Can you open the file," Ann asked.

"Sure, give me a second," he said as he clicked away on the keys.

"It looks like day-to-day notes about something. Let me read those, Matthew. Maybe they will tell us something we need to know," said Ann as she continued to read the computer screen.

MLS – If you hadn't stolen my baby, we wouldn't be having this mess to clean up.

JR – I told you I would take care of everything.

MLS – You haven't yet. She still has the boy. I want him back.

JR – Why? You don't want to have to take care of another kid.

MLS – He's my kid and I want him back.

JR – Just wait a while longer and we'll get it done through the courts.

MLS – It takes too long. I'll do it myself.

JR – No, don't do anything stupid. You could get into a lot of trouble.

MLS – You're not doing anything.

JR – Once the lawsuit gets settled for the baby mix-up, we can get the boy and more money. You just have to be patient.

MLS – How long is that going to take?

JR – A few months at the most.

"Is there another file, Matthew," asked Ann.

"Not that I could find but I'll keep looking," answered Matthew.

I can figure out who MLS is. That has to be Lillian. Who is JR? Ann wondered as she walked toward the stacked boxes.

There were fifty gallon drums stacked at the end of the boxes closest to the corner. She knew she couldn't move those monsters. *The boxes – she needed to move the boxes.*

"Mom, I found another file," shouted Matthew.

"I'll be right there," said Ann as she started walking across the large warehouse floor.

"Why would they put this stuff on my computer," asked Matthew.

When Ann had reached the area behind Matthew's chair, she said, "It's looks like someone was transcribing some tapes. Someone had tape recorded the conversations and then decided they needed all of the words down on paper. That sounds like something a black mailer would do; maybe even a lawyer."

JR – We have both of them.

MLS – What are you going to do now?

JR – Hold them until after the hearing on the boy. You will have to go to court and act like you know nothing about what is going on so you can get custody of the boy which will most likely happen because you are his biological mother. Anyway, his adopted mother won't be there because we still have her.

MLS – The hearing is next week. Will it be over after that?

JR – Yes, the settlement with Hyeres Medical Center is almost complete. Just a matter of signatures on the dotted lines and the writing of the checks. All of the parties are in agreement. You will be a rich woman.

MLS – We will be a rich couple.

JR – Yes, I meant to say that. Just a slip of the tongue.

MLS – What will happen to her, the boy's adopted

mother?

JR – She will have to have an unfortunate accident.

MLS – What about the boy?

JR – He will be at the hearing and you will be able to leave with him in your custody.

MLS – How can you be sure that will be the judge's decision?

JR – You're his biological mother.

Ann stopped reading at that point. She knew who JR was. He was Jeff's best friend. *How could he do that to Jeff and me,* she thought as she stared off into space.

"You didn't finish reading it, Mom," said Matthew when he glanced at Ann.

"I don't need to read any more of it right now," said Ann.

"Mom, I think they are going to kill you," cried Matthew.

"They aren't going to get a chance. You and I will get out of here," Ann said as she hugged her son protectively.

CHAPTER 20

DID YOU RECOGNIZE HIM?

Right after the local uniformed officers appeared at the Logan home, Detective White presented himself to Jeff.

"You said you saw the burglar, is that right," asked the detective.

"Yes sir," answered Jeff.

"Did you recognize him?"

"I thought I did but I think maybe I was wrong," said Jeff as he shook his head in emphasis.

"Why would you think that, Mr. Logan," asked the detective.

"When I was chasing him, I completely lost track of him. If he had been my neighbor, I would have seen him running to the house across the street," explained Jeff.

"Not if he didn't want you to know he was your neighbor doing the stealing. He would have gone in the opposite direction to convince you of that and it appears that he has done just that. Why did you think it was your neighbor," probed the detective.

"The long scraggily hair under the baseball hat he was wearing. His general appearance of being a street person, homeless, unclean, whatever," said Jeff defensively.

"Does your neighbor look like that," asked the detective.

"Yes, he does," answered Jeff.

"How well do you know your neighbor," asked the detective.

"I don't know him. I met him today when I knocked on his door to ask him if he had seen Ann and Matthew leave the house with someone. Of course, he rudely told me 'no,'" said Jeff.

"Mr. Logan, I would go with your first hunch. You thought it was your neighbor so that is who we are going to check out," said Detective White. "We need a list of everything that was taken. We want to get a search warrant and we need to list the items we will be searching for when we approach your neighbor."

"As far as I could tell, it was just a computer and some clothes. The only reason I know the clothes were taken is because of the way he ransacked both bedrooms looking for them. It seems strange to me, but that was all that is missing. Why do you think they took those items," asked Jeff.

"They were clothes for both your son and your wife weren't they," asked the detective.

"Yes sir," answered Jeff.

"It appears to me that someone is trying to make your family comfortable and the computer could have been taken for information purposes," suggested the detective.

"That means they probably won't kill them if they are trying to make them comfortable. Don't you think that, Detective White," asked an excited Jeff.

"I hope that's the case, Mr. Logan. If you will excuse me, I will be going to question your neighbors - all of them," said Detective White as he walked away toward the street.

Jeff watched him as he crossed the street and pounded on the door. There was no answer, no one appeared to be home so that made Jeff think maybe his hunch was right. Perhaps it was his neighbor. *But how were they going to find out?*

When the policemen finally cleared out again, Jeff made it his mission to keep an eye on the house across the street.

CHAPTER 21

WHAT DO THEY WANT?

"Matthew, come over here and help me move some of these boxes. I am pretty sure there is a door or a window back behind them," Ann said as she motioned for her son to join her.

"How are we going to do this," asked Matthew as he stood next to Ann looking at the oversized cartons.

"Let's see if we can work ourselves behind the boxes on this end because this is where the breeze is coming from," Ann said as she approached the boxes. "Let's see. You start tugging on the box at the bottom. I'll pull on the same box a little over your head. With the two of us pulling, we might get it to move a little. Then I will try to wedge myself in there so I can brace my back against the wall and push with my feet and legs. I don't know if I can do that, but I want to try," said Ann as she fought the urge to cry.

"Okay, let's do it. Count to three, Mom, and then we can both pull."

"One – two – three - pull," said Ann.

"It didn't move."

"Let's do it again. One – two – three - pull," said Ann as she strained as hard as she could.

"It moved a little bit," said Matthew excitedly.

"Again, one – two – three - pull," said Ann.

"It's moving, mom."

"Let me see if I can get behind that set of boxes," said Ann as she flattened herself against the wall to wedge herself between the wall and the boxes.

"Almost, Matthew. I can almost get behind there. Let's pull again."

The word 'almost' seemed to inspire the two of them. They both put their heart and soul into the possibility of getting out of that warehouse. Both of them would be alive and kicking at the end of the day, hopefully.

They pulled and pulled until they worked that stack of boxes away from the wall so Ann could get behind them. There were more stacks to move before she would arrive at the area where she thought the door would be.

Pushing the boxes from behind seemed to be a lot easier than pulling. They both could get a stronger momentum going and they could inch their way closer and closer to the possibility of escape.

"Matthew, I see it. Just one more stack of boxes. Let's hurry before our keeper gets back," Ann said excitedly.

They heard the keys rattle against the metal door.

"Mom, get out of there. He's unlocking the door," whispered Matthew.

Ann slid from behind the boxes and pushed Matthew to the area where they slept. He sat in front of the computer where he had a game loaded and ready to go.

Ann sat on the pile of bags, took a deep breath, and tried to be calm. She was having a difficult time trying to control her breathing because she was a bit panicky. She felt the panic moving over her the moment she sprawled out on the burlap bags. She made her mind focus on calm of ocean waves gentle and consistent; calm, calm, calm.

"Ma'am, I've brought some food. It isn't much but it will help some to keep your bellies from growling," he said with a sadness dulling his eyes.

"What is it," asked Ann. She knew she had to keep him off balance so he would not notice that the boxes had been moved. At first glance, he wouldn't have noticed the change but if he walked closer to the boxes, he would be able to see that they weren't positioned as they had previously been.

"Some packaged cheese and crackers along with a couple of cans of soda pop. It will tide you over until…" he said without finishing the sentence.

"Tide us over until what," demanded Ann.

The question must have taken the keeper by surprise. His face reddened and he sputtered a few seconds before speaking.

"What are you talking about," he said when he was finally able to form words.

"Until what? This junk you gave us to eat is supposed to tide us over until what," she screamed at him.

"Until they get what they want," he snapped.

"What do they want," Ann returned in a scream.

"Just eat your food and be glad that you are still alive."

Now, it was Ann's turn to change colors but she did not brighten to a crimson, she blanched to sheet white.

130

Before she could form another word to say, the keeper was out of the door and she could hear the lock snapping into place.

If Jeff had been close by, she would have just crumbled physically and mentally allowing him to take complete control of the situation. It had always been easier that way. He wanted to be the dominant, controlling husband. She was relegated to the role of the weak wife subjected to pills to help her keep going and she played it well.

Ann had to be strong, willful, and ready to do whatever it took to keep both her and Matthew alive and in their family of three.

"Matthew, let's get busy. We are running out of time," she whispered.

They returned to the boxes where Ann slid behind the last set of cartons she needed to move before she could reach the door.

Matthew got behind the boxes alongside of her because there was no way for him to position himself to pull the boxes. The boxes were sitting too close together, side by side, for that to happen.

He squirmed until he got his small body on the floor with his knees bent up. He braced his back against the wall and shoved with his legs and feet every time his mother said 'three.'

Ann was turning herself and shoving with her hip as she braced herself against the floor and the side wall. Ann's muscles were screaming from overuse. She knew Matthew had to be near exhaustion.

"Just a little more, baby," she whispered.

She didn't know what was in those boxes. She did know that they were stacked too high and the stack towered over both of them. If one of them fell over flat on top of them, they would be crushed.

"Almost. One more push, Matthew," she whispered weakly as she braced herself again.

She felt it move; not the box she was pushing. It was the top box and it was wobbling back to come down and cover them.

"Stay down, Matthew," she whispered.

Ann fell to the side covering Matthew with her body. She waited for the crush.

The top box leaned enough to hit the wall but because the bottom box was still so close to the wall, it couldn't continue the fall to crush them beneath.

"Matthew, are you okay," asked Ann as she fought back a sob.

"Yeah, but you are mashing me," he said breathlessly.

"I'll try to move closer to the door. If I can't, you're going to have to crawl over me and see if you can get it open," she whispered sternly so he wouldn't question her instructions.

She needed to get out from under the leaning box. If she could do that, she might be able to get herself upright again.

She started wiggling, trying to scoot off of her son's legs that had been braced against the bottom box.

"You're hurting me," said Matthew as he pushed against his mother.

"I'm sorry but I've got to scoot to the side so we can get out from under the box," she whispered as she continued to try to inch backward, feet first.

"Mom, let me try to pull my legs free," he said as he fought the tears welling up in his eyes.

"Okay. I'll brace myself as close to the box as I can get so you can back up to the wall. If you work your legs toward the way we got in here, I think you can get yourself free," she said as she moved an inch or two closer to the box.

Matthew squirmed and pushed and pulled as he tried to force himself free from his pinned position.

"I've got one leg out. Now let's get the other one," he said as he pulled on the leg with both hands trying to free it from beneath Ann's body. "Okay, it's free," he said as he cried out the words. "Can you move, Mom?"

Ann tried to scoot but she couldn't move any further.

"Crawl over me, Matthew. Go to the door and try to open it," instructed Ann.

Matthew started moving to try to get himself turned from facing the path into the area behind the boxes to work his body into the position to crawl across his mother.

Ann knew she was going to have some bruises and abrasions when he had completed his crawl but that was fine as long as they could get out of the warehouse.

"Hurry, honey, I don't know when the man will be back to kill me," Ann whispered as she tried to get him to move a bit faster.

It worked.

Matthew gave his mission his full and complete attention.

He kicked and squirmed and wiggled for what seemed like forever as he fought his way to the door and off of his mother's body.

Ann tried not to cry out every time his kick connected with some part of her body. The kicking first started with her head, then moved to her back, and on down her legs. The hardest kicks landed on her head and back.

"Can you get to the door," she asked.

"I think so. What if I can't get it open? What then," asked a scared Matthew.

"Go, Matthew, just go. See if you can open the door," she hissed as she tried not to become angry.

She could hear him making his way to the door.

Then – she heard him push the door open. It squeaked loudly when he shoved it open.

CHAPTER 22

HE HAD A GUT FEELING

Jeff wanted so much to go out looking for his family but he had no idea where to start the search.

Both he and Detective White thought that his neighbor across the street was involved so he decided to play the odds and watch the comings and goings of his neighbor.

He went outside to turn his car around facing the street so he could drive off of his driveway rather than backing up, turning, and then driving because that would waste valuable seconds. He left the driver door unlocked and pulled his flashlight from the side pocket of the door. He loaded in bottles of water and snacks. He also threw in an empty jar for bathroom duties along with some hand sanitizer and paper towels. He wanted to be prepared for whatever happened.

He knew he couldn't plant himself on the front porch waiting for his neighbor to get home. That would be too obvious.

He moved the recliner close to the front window, not straight on because someone would be able to see him. He was off to the side with a clear view of the neighbor's driveway and front door.

All he could do now was wait.

He would not allow himself to stretch out on the recliner. He was so tired that he was afraid he would fall asleep. He was sitting bolt upright but he was becoming so very drowsy.

"Coffee, coffee, I need coffee," he chanted as he rose from the recliner.

Within minutes he had the coffee brewed and he was sipping on a cup of rejuvenation. He walked back to the recliner and continued his watching.

"There he is," Jeff mumbled as he watched his neighbor pull slowly onto his driveway. To Jeff, it seemed that his neighbor did not want to draw attention to himself. He normally would have screeched onto his driveway.

Jeff watched the car door swing open and his neighbor climbed out of the vehicle. He was not carrying anything. He didn't appear to be bloody. He did not look any more disheveled than he ordinarily did. He appeared as though everything were normal.

Jeff's neighbor watching was disrupted by his ringing telephone.

"Hello," he shouted. He had no idea why he was shouting but that was what he was doing.

"Mr. Logan?"

"Yes, who is this," he said as he continued to shout.

"This is Detective White. Is there a problem now at your house," asked the concerned detective.

"No, other than my missing family. Why do you ask," he
136

shouted.

"Because you are yelling," said the detective.

"Oh, I'm sorry, detective. I didn't realize I was doing that. What do you need," asked Jeff as he lowered his voice volume.

"Have you seen any sign of your neighbor," the detective asked.

"Yes, he just arrived home."

"I don't want you to do anything except keep watch from your house. I will be on my way momentarily to question him," instructed Detective White.

"Okay, no problem. I'm watching him."

"Nothing else, Mr. Logan, just watch him from your house. I will be on my way."

"Yes sir," said Jeff.

As soon as he disconnected the call, his neighbor walked out the front door carrying a rifle and a large plastic bag filled with items that appeared to be heavy.

Jeff stood up so he could get a better look down the road but there was no sign of Detective White's vehicle.

Jeff grabbed his car keys and stood next to his open front door as he watched his neighbor back out of his driveway.

Still no sign of Detective White.

Jeff ran out the door as soon as his neighbor started driving down the street. Jeff pulled off of his driveway while his neighbor's car was still in sight. He continued to scan the oncoming traffic for Detective White but he made sure he was following behind his neighbor.

"What am I going to do if he leads me to where he is keeping Ann and Matthew," he mumbled. Talking to himself was helping him settle on each of his next steps. He didn't care whether or not anyone thought he was crazy.

Suddenly his neighbor turned his vehicle to the right onto a dead end street. Jeff knew there were warehouses on that street. Some of those warehouses were abandoned and would be a great place to hide hostages.

He drove on past the street where his neighbor turned off. He pulled to the side of the street he was on and parked. Jeff exited his vehicle, glanced around for identifying objects, and walked casually toward the dead end street.

He didn't want to appear anxious and scared so he tucked his hands into his pockets and tilted his head down but not so far that he couldn't see what was happening around him.

He had a gut feeling that he was where he needed to be - *but why?*

He continued to walk, glancing around to look for human activity. When he arrived at the dead end of the street, he was standing in front of a huge warehouse.

One half of the warehouse was closed, locked up, and unused; or, at least, that was how it looked. The other half was in better condition. He could see some interior lighting through the dirty, streaked windows and he could hear the sound of some kind of engine coming from inside. Perhaps it was a fork lift running. He just wasn't sure.

He walked toward the unused side of the warehouse. He couldn't explain why he was heading in that direction. He felt he had to go that way.

Jeff spotted the lock hanging from the hasp and it was closed.

"Now what," he asked himself.

He walked around to the back of the building and there he spotted his neighbor's car. He stopped abruptly. He didn't want his neighbor to see him standing there.

The car looked empty and that meant that his neighbor was out walking around somewhere and that there was a likelihood that he would spot Jeff.

The thought that he should have waited for Detective White raced through his brain. *No,* his thought continued, *if I had waited, I wouldn't know where the neighbor had driven and I know Ann and Matthew are here. I know they are here.*

He pulled his cell phone from his pocket. He was going to call Detective White and tell him his location and why he was there.

"No service."

Jeff knew there were certain parts of the town that were cut off from cell service due to the surrounding terrain but he had no idea he was standing in the middle of a dead zone.

"Now what," he mumbled again.

He turned away from the warehouse and started walking. When he reached his car, he climbed in and settled himself to wait, once again.

He had parked his vehicle so he would be facing away from the street leading to the warehouse. He used his rearview mirror to watch for his neighbor to leave the area. He checked his cell phone again.

"No service."

CHAPTER 23

WHAT IS ON THE OTHER SIDE?

"Matthew, does the door lock automatically when you close it," Ann whispered.

"I think so," he answered,

"Take your shoe off and wedge it between the door and the facing. Do you understand what I'm saying," asked Ann hurriedly.

"Yes, I did it. Now what," he asked.

"Take a peek outside that door and tell me what is on the other side," Ann said.

Matthew pushed the door open making sure his shoe stayed put. He walked to the other side and discovered he was in another building. In this building, he could hear people talking and moving around on some kind of machine.

He ran back to the door, opened it, and squeezed back inside.

"Mom, there is another building on the other side of the door. There are people in there. I could hear some kind of machine. What do you want me to do," he asked excitedly.

"Help me get out of here. You grab my legs and pull. I'll

140

brace myself up a bit and push with my arms. Can you do that," she asked skeptically.

"I don't want to hurt you, mom," he said tearfully.

"You have to do this, Matthew. Please help me, please," Ann whispered tearfully.

Matthew leaned over and grabbed hold of his mother's legs. He held them at each side of his body and waited for her signal.

"Pull, Matthew," Ann whispered harshly.

As he pulled on her lifted legs, she used all the strength she could gather into her arms and pushed herself backwards between the wall and the boxes.

"Do it again, baby," she whispered followed by the word, "Pull!"

A little more progress. She had moved a little closer to the door.

"Just one more time, Matthew. Then I think I will be close enough to the door to work my way to it so I can stand up. Pull," she said in barely a whisper.

Ann pushed herself back far enough to be out from under the leaning box. She wiggled her hips forcing herself to move inch by inch to the door. When she knew her legs were free of the box in front of the door, she knew she would be able to stand upright again.

"Matthew, hold the door open a bit so I can back out from this hole," instructed Ann.

Ann felt her legs free up. She wiggled some more to get her hips out of the confining space. She had to twist and turn a bit to free up her shoulders. She backed up forcing her rear end up into the air, then she pulled herself upright using the door and Matthew as her braces.

She took a deep breath and almost fell to her knees from exhaustion. She grabbed for the door again and she pushed it open far enough so that the two of them could leave their prison.

CHAPTER 24

THE LIGHT WAS BEGINNING TO FADE

Jeff watched his neighbor's car leave the street leading to the warehouse. He started his vehicle and searched for a place to turn around so he could drive up and behind the warehouse.

He sat there in his car looking around, observing, waiting for someone to come out of the bushes, spring at him, and kill him.

The light was beginning to fade and the warehouse activity was coming to a halt.

He exited his car and walked around to the front of the opened end of the building where he stood close to the front entrance.

He watched as a couple of men left who were dressed in blue jeans and tee shirts, employees he assumed. He poked his head around the side of the door to get a glimpse. No one was near the doorway so he slipped inside keeping his backside against the wall as close as he could so he could hide in the darker fringes of the building.

The overhead lights went out and he stood there staring into the darkness waiting for his eyes to adjust so he could walk deeper into the building.

In his heart he knew Ann and Matthew were near. He had to keep looking. He had to find them.

***

Ann and Matthew cowered behind some shelves that were positioned so that they were about two feet from the wall near the door that had led them into that side of the building.

It wasn't hard to keep Matthew quiet. He was as scared as she was. She was so afraid her keeper and potential killer would return to find them gone and follow their trail from captivity that would lead directly to where they were cowering in fear, waiting for a chance to escape.

The overhead lights went out and she realized it was about time to make a move.

"Mom, I'm scared," whispered Matthew.

"Me, too," whispered Ann. "It will be okay when we get out of here. Just wait for a little bit to let your eyes adjust to the darkness, and then we will try to move to the door. Okay?"

Matthew didn't respond but she knew he nodded his head in agreement.

She was starting to distinguish shapes in the darkness.

"Can you see now, Matthew," she whispered.

"A little bit. Are we going to leave now," he asked in a voice louder than he should have.

"Sh-sh-sh-sh," Ann said.

Ann grabbed Matthew's hand and started moving to where she thought the door would be. It was a slow go. Even though she could distinguish shapes of objects that were sitting further out

144

from the wall, she wasn't able to see the smaller pieces of debris that were right in front of her. The darkness would swallow them up leaving them as obstacles to trip over causing her to bang up her shins, knees, and toes.

She tried to ignore the pain radiating from her shins as she directed Matthew around the obstacle.

***

Jeff worked his way to where he thought there might be an entrance into the other half of the building.

He was dragging his back against whatever it was that was attached to the walls. He felt the spider webs and dirt attaching to his clothes as if he had a magnet in the weave of the cloth.

The warehouse was completely quiet.

No – there was a noise just a little beyond where he was moving.

He stopped and was perfectly still, immobile.

He didn't hear anything so he started moving again, staying flat against the wall.

***

Ann heard a noise that she and Matthew hadn't made.

She stopped to listen.

Nothing – no noise.

She continued on.

"Mom, how much further," asked Matthew whose patience was wearing thin.

"I don't know, but I think we're getting close," Ann whispered.

The noise – she heard it again.

"Do you see anyone moving around, Matthew," whispered Ann.

"No, but I keep hearing a sliding sound," he answered.

"I do, too. It sounds like something brushing against a wall. Let's keep moving. I want to find that door and get out of here," Ann said.

***

Jeff could hear voices. He couldn't make out the words but he definitely could hear voices. They didn't sound like the workers.

"Ann? Matthew," he whispered. "Ann, it's Jeff. Are you in here? If you are, where are you?"

Ann tilted her head to try to catch the whisper that was riding the air waves in the warehouse.

"Jeff," she answered. "Over here, next to the wall."

"Stay there, I'm coming to you. Is Matthew with you," he asked.

"I'm here, dad. I'm right beside mom. Help us, please," Matthew said tearfully.

Jeff took an excited, deep breath. He couldn't believe he had found them. He continued to slide against the nasty, dirty wall to find his wife and son.

"Ann? I think I can see you," he whispered.

"I see you, Jeff. Matthew is right beside me," Ann said.

"Stay there. I'll be right there," he whispered.

Finally, they were standing side by side, backs up against the wall, and not moving except for the smile on each of their faces.

146

"What do we do now," Ann asked Jeff.

"You two follow me to the front door. I don't think there is anyone in here but we can't take a chance on getting caught trying to escape so we've still got to be quiet. Okay," he whispered.

"Yes, okay," answered Ann.

Jeff grabbed Ann's hand as she held onto Matthew's hand.

"Wait a second, Jeff. Let's put Matthew in the middle," said Ann cautiously.

Ann pulled Matthew forward and she grabbed one hand as Jeff grabbed onto the other. Jeff led them closer to the entrance and to safety.

"Sh-sh-sh-sh, I hear a car," said Jeff.

The vehicle tires, car or whatever, was crunching the ground in front of the building. Two slams from the vehicle doors were heard along with voices.

"They are coming in here," whispered Ann fearfully.

"I know. Just stay where you are and don't make a sound," cautioned Jeff.

The crunching sound of the gravel stopped, the vehicle engine roared to life, and the movement of the vehicle could be heard close to the building and driving around to the backside where Jeff had parked his car.

"They are going to find my car and they will know I'm around here looking for you," Jeff whispered.

"Oh, no," said Ann. "What do we do now?"

"We keep moving. Maybe we can get out of here before they get back to this end of the building," said Jeff as he moved toward the front entrance.

After a few moments, they could hear voices again filtering through from the other side of the building.

"They have discovered we aren't there," said Ann who was so frightened she could barely move. "They are planning to kill both of us, Jeff, and take Matthew away."

"We'll see about that," said Jeff as he pulled out his cell phone.

'No service' popped up again on the small screen. He moved it around several times, thrusting it into the air, but it didn't help.

"Maybe we can find a land line in the front of the building. After all, this is a business. They would need some kind of phone," he mumbled.

"They are probably just using cell phones for business purposes," said Ann.

"They can't. There is no service here," snapped Jeff.

"Okay, let's go find a phone," said Ann in a calming tone.

They moved on to the front where Jeff tried the door. Of course, it was locked from the outside, probably with a padlock.

"Let's look in the office," Jeff said as he led them away from the front of the building to a square shaped cubicle of an office against the opposite wall.

"The door is locked," said Matthew.

"I'll open it. Move over here, son," said Jeff as he banged against it with his hip followed by a thrust of his foot.

The door flew open with a loud bang against the wall and they all three rushed inside to find a phone.

Jeff knew the noise he had been making was going to attract attention from the owner of the voices on the other side of the building, but he still had to take that chance.

"Here it is," whispered Matthew as he handed the receiver to Jeff. The face of the receiver of the cordless telephone lit up so he could see the numbers to dial 9-1-1.

"Hello, this is Jeff Logan. Please tell Detective White I have found Ann and Matthew and the kidnappers are planning to kill us. We are hiding in a warehouse at the end of Depot Street. Please send help," he said as he disconnected the line.

"All right, guys," Jeff said to his family. "Find a place where you can duck down and hide. I'm going to close this door and let them think we are gone. Ann, you get under the desk. Matthew, you get under that table and pull some boxes over in front of you. I'll go behind those file cabinets. Don't make a sound. They are getting closer to us."

Jeff held his breath as did Matthew and Ann as they strained to hear the voices of the people searching the space where they had been hiding.

"Jeff," said Ann.

"What," he whispered.

"That voice is familiar," said Ann.

"I know. I've heard it before but I can't put my finger on it," said Jeff.

"It's Mr. Richards," said Matthew. "Maybe he is here to help us."

"Keep your voice down, Matthew. I don't think it is Joe and I don't think they are going to help us," whispered Jeff.

Jeff could hear the voices more clearly and much to his dismay, he discovered that Matthew was right. It was the voice of Joe Richards, his attorney.

He, Ann, and Matthew had been betrayed – big time.

The voices were getting closer and Jeff was getting nervous.

"Where did they go? They didn't get out of here. The car is still parked out back," said Joe Richards.

"They've got to be in here somewhere. I know they didn't get out. I don't know how a kid and sickly woman managed to move those boxes. I needed help to get them in front of the door," snarled the second man who Jeff thought was their neighbor.

"Did you check in there," asked Joe as he pointed to the office.

"No, it's supposed to be locked up tight," said the neighbor.

Joe walked to the door and rattled the knob. The door popped open and Joe walked inside placing his hand against the wall to search for a light switch.

Jeff sucked in a breath. He was afraid to breathe, afraid he would be heard.

Joe stood for a moment as his eyes adjusted to the brightness of the overhead fluorescents. He didn't move as he glanced around the small office searching for Jeff, Ann, and Matthew. He turned to leave the office.

"Nobody in here," he shouted to the second man.

He walked through the doorway pulling the door closed behind him.

Jeff exhaled and felt his knees try to buckle under him. He did not step out of his hiding place until he heard them leave the building.

"Ann, Matthew, you can come out now," he whispered.

Slowly Ann left the knee hole space under the desk and

Matthew crawled out of hiding behind the boxes that were in front of the table he was beneath.

"You were right, Matthew, it was Joe Richards. And the man with him was our neighbor that lives across the street from our house," said Jeff.

Ann walked up to Jeff and put her arms around him.

"I'm so sorry it is your friend. Why do you think he is doing this," she asked softly.

"I don't have a clue but I think he is in cahoots with Lillian. I guess it's all of the money they are after from Hyeres Medical Center and Matthew. They have to have Matthew as proof of the baby switch especially since the other boy died and was cremated," explained Jeff.

"That sounds about right," said Ann.

"What other explanation could there be," asked Jeff.

"Mom? Dad? Are we going to get out of here," asked Matthew.

"Not until I hear the vehicle start that will take them away from here. They are probably still looking outside for signs of where we went," Jeff said.

An engine roaring to life caused the warehouse walls to vibrate. The crunching of gravel seemed to last forever as the vehicle encircled the huge structure before fading as it drove away from them.

"It's gone, dad," said Matthew.

"Give it a couple more minutes to see if they come back," suggested Jeff.

The three of them stood huddled together as they waited.

"Let's see if we can get out of here now. I don't hear anything except us. We will probably have to break the door down to get out," he said as they started walking across the warehouse.

As they got closer to the door, Jeff was getting the feeling that something wasn't right.

Why hadn't Joe checked further into the office? Maybe he saw something. Maybe he heard one of us breathing. Why did he just turn and leave?

"Slow down, Matthew. Let me go first," instructed Jeff.

"Ann, something's not right about this. I'm afraid Joe has made it too easy for us," he whispered.

"I think you're right. What should we do," she asked.

"The only thing we can do is go out that door no matter what is waiting for us outside. Matthew, get behind me and stay there," he said sternly.

Matthew did as he was told.

Jeff reached for the door knob and it turned easily.

"This is not good," he mumbled as he pushed the door open slowly.

Suddenly the door was jerked away from Jeff as Joe aimed a handgun at Jeff's heart.

"Come on out, Jeff; you, too, Ann," said Joe as he kept his gun leveled for a direct hit at Jeff's sternum.

"Matthew, you run over there and get into that car," said Joe as he motioned the gun toward the parked SUV.

"No, not without my mom and dad," said a tearful Matthew.

"Now, kid, get over there now. Your mom and dad will be

there as soon as we have a little talk," said Joe as he tried not to sound angry but failed to achieve his goal.

Matthew moved slowly.

"Move it, kid," shouted Joe.

Matthew took off running.

"Get that kid," shouted Joe as he looked at the second man.

The neighbor took off running after Matthew but his pace was much slower than Matthew's.

"I'll never catch that kid," he shouted as he ran.

"If you want your money, you've got to grab him and bring him back here," said Joe angrily.

He motioned for Ann to move out from behind Jeff so he could see what she was doing.

"You two are causing more trouble than you are worth," he hissed angrily. "Back up and get inside the building."

"Why? What are you going to do," asked Ann.

"What I should have done in the very beginning," he snarled. "Now move it. Don't try anything stupid or I will shoot you. It is just as easy to shoot you now than it is later. I just don't want to have to move your bodies in the daylight. Now, turn around and walk back into the building. Keep your hands up where I can see them."

Jeff was trying hard to figure out his next move but nothing came to mind. Ann was wilting mentally and physically with all of the effort she had already put forth to survive and now it was coming to an end. It was the ending she had tried so very hard to avoid.

"What are you going to do with Matthew," asked Ann as she

tried to control her tears.

"He is going back to his mother, his real mother," said Joe Richards.

"Why are you helping her and not us? What kind of hold does she have over you," demanded Jeff.

"I guess it doesn't matter if I tell you now, so here it is. Matthew is my son and I want all of the money that is going to go to Lillian and Matthew. Eventually, all of it will be mine alone," he said smugly.

"What about your helper who is out there looking for Matthew? Are you going to kill him, too," asked Jeff as he was trying to keep Joe Richards talking and away from the thoughts of pulling the trigger.

"I'll pay him off. If that doesn't work, I will eliminate the problem. You get my drift, don't you, my good old best buddy," Joe said with an ugly laugh.

"You knew all along that my son was your son. That is why you facilitated our friendship. That is why you wanted to be my best friend so you could keep an eye on him and the money he represented," said Jeff as he was trying to puzzle out this whole mess.

"I just wanted to keep an eye on him at first but when money became involved, I became more interested. I knew about the baby switch. I did it or had it done by one of the hospital employees who needed my legal services and who has since died in a car accident. I didn't want Lillian to have control of my son. She wouldn't have taken care of him like I knew you would. Now, you've got the why and how, are you happy," he smirked.

"Yes," said Jeff. "I really needed to know all of this so I could explain it when I go to the hearing next week."

"You are not going to live that long," snarled Joe.

Standing inside the warehouse put them all in the shadows with the only light filtering in from the open door.

Joe Richards had positioned himself with his back to the doorway so Jeff and Ann would not be able to escape without knocking him down. In so doing, he could not see the events that were occurring beyond the doorway.

Jeff had kept him talking long enough to allow the police who were arriving on foot to encircle the building.

Joe Richards heard the footfalls of someone coming up behind him.

"Did you find the kid," Joe asked as he assumed the neighbor was approaching from the rear.

"Yeah, we did," came the gruff answer that definitely was not the neighbor.

Joe Richards whirled around, gun in hand, and was shot right where he stood, falling to the feet of Jeff and Ann.

Jeff reached out to embrace his wife's shaking, sobbing body. He needed to help her survive this ordeal but he needed her help to survive as well.

"Matthew," screamed Ann between sobs. "Where is Matthew?"

"Right here, Mrs. Logan. He is the hero. He helped me set this up. You've got a smart boy there."

"Yes sir, we know that. He is our boy, our son, our Matthew," said Jeff as he hugged Ann and Matthew vowing to never let them go.

"The other guy, did you get him," asked Jeff when he saw Detective White.

"Yes, and he is singing like a canary. Seems he was forced

into everything he did by Mr. Richards who was his attorney on a drug dealing charge that was going to put him away for many years," explained the detective.

"I knew he was involved, but I had no idea Joe Richards, my best friend, was the instigator of this whole mess."

CHAPTER 25

THE DAY OF THE HEARING ARRIVES

"Jeff, are you awake," Ann asked tugging at his arm.

"Yes I'm awake. Your tossing and turning in bed last night and that 'all you can eat pizza' we had at Jenna's Italian Restaurant, kept my stomach churning most of the night," Jeff said as he turned toward Ann in the bed.

"The hearing is supposed to start at 1 p.m.. There should be no problem at all with this court appearance, you know. Of course, we won't have a lawyer representing us but we have to go anyway. It is just a formality, I hope," said Ann as she crawled across the bed to get her lazy husband up and moving.

"I wonder if Lillian was arrested. What part did she play in the baby-switching, kidnapping, and murder plan? Will she be at the hearing? I meant to ask Detective White the last time we spoke, but it slipped my mind," said Jeff as he pondered all the unanswered questions that were roaming around in his mind.

"Do you think she will be there? At the hearing, I mean. Do you think she will show up," asked Ann as worry clouded her previously smiling face.

"She is the plaintiff or complainant, the person who is making the charges. She would have to be there unless she was arrested. If she didn't show up, she would lose automatically if she didn't have a good reason for not being there," explained Jeff.

"I hope she doesn't show up, don't you," asked Ann.

"Yes, that would make our life a little bit easier," said Jeff.

"I'm going to go wake up Matthew so he can get awake and ready for the day," said Ann as she left the bedroom.

Jeff ducked into the bathroom to take a shower. When he completed his bathroom duties, he expected Ann to take her turn in the bathroom but she wasn't in the bedroom.

He finished with his dressing requirements and went in search of Ann.

"Ann? The bathroom is clear now," he shouted as he walked through the hallway.

When he received no answer, he poked his head into Matthew's room and found him still asleep.

"Matthew, time to get up," he told his son from across the room. "Has your mother been in here?"

Matthew yawned, stretched, and answered, "No."

"Get up, okay Buddy," said Jeff as he walked to the doorway. "I'm going to go find your mom."

Jeff slowly descended the stairs almost afraid of what he might find. It was unlike Ann to forget to wake up Matthew. He knew something was wrong, terribly wrong.

When he reached the bottom of the staircase, he paused to listen for sounds of movement.

Nothing – no sounds – no one moving around to prepare breakfast.

There was a chill racing down his spine.

Not again, he thought as he took a step towards the living room.

He saw the barrel of a gun extending beyond the partition that separated the living room from the kitchen.

He stopped forward movement again as he tried to figure out what to do next.

I need to tell Matthew to stay upstairs, thought Jeff as he gently started up the staircase.

"Stop," shouted a somewhat familiar, female voice.

Jeff halted in mid-step.

"What do you want, Lillian?"

"My son, where is my son," she said harshly. "Get over here, Ann, so I can keep an eye on both of you."

Ann shuffled into the foyer with a disgusted look on her face.

"I'm so sorry, Jeff," she mumbled.

"Why are you sorry," asked Jeff.

Ann didn't answer. She cast her glance to her feet and sighed.

"What do you want," Jeff asked as he looked at Lillian.

"My son and the money the hospital owes me for this mistake," Lillian said.

"Do you really think you are going to win this case," asked Jeff.

"Yes, I am his mother," Lillian hissed.

"You aren't his mother. I'm his mother. All you did was give him birth. That does not make you a mother," Ann said hotly.

"According to the laws of the state, it does make me his mother, his legal mother," snapped Lillian.

"Then it's an unjust law in an unjust court. That can't happen, Lillian. You are a criminal and we legally are the parents of Matthew. Our names appear on the birth certificate, not yours," said Jeff loudly and sternly.

That statement struck a sour note with Lillian. She straightened up, standing tall and frightening as she tightened her grip on the handgun she was holding with both hands. Her gaze was straight at Jeff but her gun barrel was pointed directly at Ann.

"Yes, but the babies were switched. That's why the hospital is in trouble. It was their fault. They caused the trouble," hissed Lillian in answer.

"You know the hospital had nothing to do with the switch. Joe Richards did it. Your bedmate did it. He didn't want you raising his kid," said Jeff.

"I know that. He told me about that a few years ago. I was so mad at him but I had a little boy to raise. It wasn't my little boy but I loved him. I really thought Joe lied to me until the blood tests came back that proved James wasn't my son. Now, I want my real son back," Lillian said as she tried to hide her emotions behind loud, angry words.

"You helped him plan the whole scene, didn't you," demanded Ann.

"Yes – yes – I did. I wanted what was due to me and Joe Richards was going to help me get my boy back. It was – it is his son, too. We were going to get the money and live happily ever after," Lillian said with a smirk. "Joe's in jail now. So I have to do all the dirty work. But he'll get out. I will wait for him to get out. Then me, the kid, and Joe can be happy forever."

"You know Joe was going to kill the boy and you after he got his hands on the money," Jeff said nonchalantly.

"No – no – that's a lie. We were going to be happy. We were going to live out of the country where we couldn't be extradited back to here. We were going to be happy. Just the three of us," Lillian said with a smile.

"What are you going to do to us, Lillian," asked Ann.

"Kill you, of course. I can't have you walking into that court room. You will mess everything up. The judge will have to let me have my kid. It's the law. He has to give me back my boy," Lillian said as she waved the gun around to punctuate her statement.

"No, he doesn't because our names are on the birth certificate. We are his legal parents and if something happens to us, we have designated guardians, my sister Kay and her husband Melvin, who are named in our will. You will have no legal right to claim him as your son regardless of what the DNA tests indicate. Just give it up, Lillian. I am his mother and you will never get custody," said Ann as she scowled.

Jeff looked at Ann and couldn't believe what he was hearing.

"How did you find out all of that legal stuff," he asked his amazing wife.

"The Internet, of course," Ann said as the hint of a smile appeared at the corners of her mouth.

Jeff glanced toward the staircase and saw Matthew mouthing 'police'. He realized what Matthew was trying to tell him.

The door burst open and guns entered the room followed by men clad in black S.W.A.T. suits.

"Drop the gun," screamed one of the policemen.

Lillian whirled around with the gun up and poised to shoot.

There was a flurry of gunfire and Lillian fell to the floor.

Ann screamed and Jeff ran to her to see if she had been struck by a bullet.

"No, I'm okay. I'm just so relieved. I was so scared she would do it. That crazy woman was going to kill us just like Joe Richards was planning to do. How much money was involved in that settlement? Was it enough for them to kill all of us," asked Ann.

Detective White heard the question and was prepared with the answer.

"A couple of million is what Joe Richards told me. You didn't know about the amount," he asked Jeff.

"No, he said an amount had not been settled on but he thought it would be a couple hundred thousand. I thought that was a good amount but not enough to kill for," said Jeff.

"Well, you folks shouldn't be having any more custody problems. And – you need to thank that boy of yours for being on the ball and giving us a call. He told us what was going on the whole time. He stayed on the phone with us until we were set to burst through the door," said Detective White.

"Our son, Matthew Logan, is the best son anyone could ever have," said Ann as she caught Matthew when he ran to her.

OTHER BOOKS BY RODNEY SMITH

THE HARD FALL

NO WHERE TO RUN

WHO'S GOING TO BURY DADDY

THE TREE ON THE HILL

MIRANDA'S SHATTERED LIFE

A RACE TO CAPTURE THE PAST

TO STOP CORRUPTION

JOURNEY THROUGH MY MIND

OTHER BOOKS BY LINDA HOAGLAND

FICTION

SNOOPING CAN BE DOGGONE DEADLY

SNOOPING CAN BE DEVIOUS

SNOOPING CAN BE CONTAGIOUS

SNOOPING CAN BE DANGEROUS

THE BEST DARN SECRET

CROOKED ROAD STALKER

CHECKING ON THE HOUSE

DEATH BY COMPUTER

THE BACKWARDS HOUSE

AN AWFULLY LONELY PLACE

NONFICTION

90 YEARS AND STILL GOING STRONG

QUILTED MEMORIES

LIVING LIFE FOR OTHERS

JUST A COUNTY BOY: DON DUNFOR

WATCH OUT FOR EDDY

THE LITTLE OLD LADY NEXT DOOR (Out of Print)

COLLECTIONS

I AM…LINDA ELLEN

A COLLECTION OF WINNERS

Rodney Smith & Linda Hoagland

45506857R00095

Made in the USA
Charleston, SC
25 August 2015